Battle of the Wingmen

Wingman 20

Battle of the Wingmen

Wingman 20

Mack Maloney

SPEAKING VOLUMES, LLC
NAPLES, FLORIDA
2020

Battle of the Wingmen

ISBN 978-1-64540-241-1

For Lt. Colonel Thomas J. Howley, U.S. Army (ret)
Thank you for your service

PART ONE

The Ghosts Inside

Chapter One

Vatu Island
South Pacific

When what happened that day was later written down by the scribes of the Tannu tribe, the story they told would be considered too fantastic to be true.

Yet it was.

On this day, the heavenly being the tribe had been waiting for, the deity to whom they'd been praying for more than a half century, finally returned.

Only one person saw him at first. Joseph Yugo Bateri was chief of the 4,000-strong Tannu Family, native inhabitants of Vatu, one of the many Solomon Islands.

When the god reappeared, Bateri was where he was every night: atop Vatu's holy plateau, facing west, just as the sun was going down. Close by was the tribe's most sacred icon: a crude wooden statue of an airplane, the vehicle in which the god had previously descended to Earth.

When the sun went down, Chief Bateri shouldered his ceremonial stick and marched up and down the grassy plateau as it if was a parade grounds, another nightly ritual. Then he lit the twelve ceremonial torches around the airplane and settled down to pray for the night, hoping like every night for the past 60 years, the god would finally hear the pleas of his people and return to Vatu again.

And this night, he did.

The god arrived in another kind of flying machine this time.

It appeared out of the stars, a faint light that grew bigger and bigger until it was hovering right over him, bringing a great wind even though there was no wind tonight.

A powerful beam of light shot out of the aircraft, blinding Bateri, but not in any bad way. This part the myths had gotten right. He could feel its warmth just like the old books said, even though the wind was now so vicious, it was nearly blowing him off the mountain. It was tough to keep his balance, but at the same time, he was close to ecstasy.

The machine finally landed, the spinning sticks on its top slowed down and it became calm again.

But in a moment that the seers had promised would be one of intense religious frenzy, Bateri instead felt himself frozen to the spot, stunned that it was really happening.

The side of the machine opened, and the god stepped out. He was dressed all in gray, not quite as the myth had prophesied, but he was wearing a pearl-white helmet emblazoned with lightning bolts. The seers had that one absolutely right.

He approached and somehow Bateri got himself moving again. But only enough to step forward a few feet and then go down to his knees in supplication.

He began chanting the name of the deity, as the seers instructed, asking if he was in fact who they'd been waiting for.

"Are you John Fromm, sir?" Bateri sang with a trembling voice. "Are you . . . John Fromm?"

The god lifted him up off his knees and shook his hand.

"No," he said. "My name is Hawk Hunter . . ."

Chapter Two

After more than a decade of occupation, the Asian Mercenary Cult was leaving its colony in America.

It was not a withdrawal; it was a full retreat. From San Jose down to San Diego, east to Las Vegas and Phoenix, the AMC's territory had once encompassed nearly all the American Southwest. But now their troop trucks were pouring into the Port of Los Angeles from every direction, their occupants set to endure a long, dishonorable voyage back to where they came from.

Six months ago, this would have seemed impossible. But in that half year, the resurgent United Americans had expelled the Russians from New York City, had obliterated a massive Russian weapons factory on an island off Siberia and had started a firestorm in Russian-occupied Hamburg that burned down half the city. Knowing they'd be next, the AMC decided it was time to go.

They'd struck a deal with the UA. The AMC would depart peacefully, leaving the continental United States truly free of foreign invaders for the first time since World War Three.

But they would have to leave all of their military equipment behind and literally swear on their ancestors never to come back.

A proxy agreement was signed—but just to make sure, 72 hours before the AMC's deadline to leave, the UA secretly air-dropped three members of the JAWS Special Forces team into Los Angeles.

Arriving late one night via a HALO insertion, the team guided their parachutes to three separate locations around the city. Once down, each man established a hidden observation post, and from these vantage points, they were able to witness the AMC withdrawal up close.

What they saw was a massive, three-day traffic jam. The streets in and around the huge port became so clogged with AMC military vehicles, by Day 2, driving was impossible. Long columns of despondent soldiers resulted, the hot LA sun broiling them in lines unshaded while they waited for orders to board their ships.

Still, as the three JAWS members could attest, it was as orderly a bug out as could be. The only surprise was the actual number of AMC troops leaving America. Initial reports indicated somewhere in the 90,000-range. This turned out to be low. Just by doing the math of how many ships were being loaded—mostly old cruise liners, thirty-six in all—and how many weapons were being left behind, a more accurate number was north of 120,000 souls.

The JAWS spies were also quick to note that everyone they saw boarding ships was military. No families, no dependents, no one else in sight, except the broken warriors of the Asian Mercenary Cult.

As darkness fell and the moon rose heralding the third day, all was still going according to plan. The port area was bustling as the last of the AMC troops were loaded onto their boats. But cleared of civilians many weeks ago, downtown LA was now a ghost town. Its streets were full of abandoned AMC vehicles, especially around the harbor, where the worst of the widespread traffic snarl now sat, frozen in place.

But all was quiet.

Until the clock struck midnight.

It started when an AMC anti-aircraft battery located at the south end of the port, and just minutes from being abandoned, picked up an unidentified blip on its radar screen.

Something was coming in off the ocean. It was flying at just 5,000 feet, but going nearly 2,000 mph, an astounding speed for any airplane these days. In the confusion of the moment, the battery opened up on the bogie with its giant twin Bofors 44mm gun. Within a minute, every AA battery still manned around the port, more than thirty individual sites in all, started shooting at it as well.

One moment, clear, peaceful skies

The next, total chaos.

The three JAWS spies immediately began radioing each other, reporting what they were seeing. The unknown aircraft was painted all black and was flying without navigation lights, making it hard to identify its type. But that wasn't the only thing mysterious about it.

Lit by two, monstrously elongated exhaust flames, soon after arriving over the city, the aircraft began performing a series of jaw-dropping maneuvers.

Captain Jim Cook, commander of the JAWS team, was ensconced atop the 500-foot high LA City Hall building. He saw the mystery plane come to a screeching halt right over his head, decelerating from at least 1500 knots to almost nothing. Pulling its nose up, it then hung motionless for much longer than gravity should have allowed before falling back down, booting its afterburners and disappearing into the night with an earsplitting roar.

Twenty miles to the south, in Torrance, Clancy Miller, XO of the JAWS team, was stationed atop the Golden West Tower skyscraper. He saw the plane performing high-speed 360-degree turns over Redondo Beach just west of him. Cook and Clancy's reports came so close to each other, for a few minutes, the JAWS team thought there might be more than one airplane involved.

Strangest of all was the report by Mark Snyder, the third JAWS member to jump into the city. He'd set up his OP atop the Ocean Center Building in Long Beach, very close to the Port of LA where he saw the jet perform a series of mock attacks on the AMC ships at anchor inside the massive harbor. Flying at wave-top level, the mystery plane would go into an offensive profile aiming for one of the evacuation vessels before turning up on its tail at the last instant and screaming straight up until it was lost in the stars—only to come back down again and do the same thing to another ship.

The noise was deafening, turning the formerly orderly departure to bedlam. Finally, after taunting the AMC ships a half dozen times, the airplane turned west, hit its afterburners and disappeared, leaving a great sonic boom behind.

The mystery airplane was over the city for only five minutes. But in that time, it had flown through a virtual fireworks display of AA fire—and that in itself was a problem.

The AMC used two kinds of anti-aircraft weapons: twin-barrel radar-guided Bofors guns and SA-6 surface-to-air missiles. With the mystery airplane's sudden appearance, the combined AMC crews had fired more than ten tons of ordnance into the air, none of it coming close to knocking the ghostly aircraft out of the sky.

But those ten tons of expended launchers and depleted AA shells came back down to earth, creating a storm of burning, razor-sharp shrapnel to rain all over LA.

Chapter Three

Dawn broke.

The pandemonium from the night before was gone, replaced with an eerie quiet as all of Los Angeles, right down to the harbor, fell nearly silent.

Most of the fires caused by the falling debris had burned themselves out, but much smoke still remained. The streets, the sidewalks, the wharves and all of the docks in the massive port were jam packed with not just abandoned vehicles, but tons of used military equipment and many more tons of random trash. Small tornadoes of litter tore through the last of the empty spaces. The sun began warming the city's wet pavements. A faint mist rose into the morning haze.

The AMC was gone. The last of the three dozen ships left at 0500 hours, per the agreement with the UA. The unarmed convoy took three hours to form up out near Catalina Island.

Then slotting in three lines of twelve vessels each, they turned west and began the journey home.

Encamped just outside the LA city limits, near the city of Palmdale, another army lay in wait.

It was comprised of infantry units from all over the continental United States, including Football City, the Pacific American Armed Forces and the Texas Free Army. Air support was provided by six squadrons of captured Hind Mi-24N helicopter gunships, courtesy of the Army of New York City. Dozens of tanks, armored vehicles and troop trucks were also on hand, thanks to the Free Canadian Army.

There were 50,000 soldiers in all. At exactly 0600, one hour after the last AMC ship left, and with the sun now fully up, they marched into the city.

At just about the same time, in the waters south of LA, the silhouette of an enormous warship appeared on the horizon. Even from twenty miles away it was obvious the vessel was a colossus.

It was the aircraft carrier, USS *USA*. Nearly a quarter mile long and almost a football field wide, it had transited the Panama Canal two days before, after leaving New York City two weeks before that. The journey was not without its perils, but in the end it was a success.

This giant vessel was built several years earlier by elements inside the New Russian Empire, and it was no idle boast that it was the most powerful warship in the world. It was probably the most powerful warship ever built—and it now belonged to the United Americans.

They'd captured it from the Russians not a year before during the Battle of New York City. It had seen action twice since, both times in the Atlantic, both times serving as a launch and recovery platform for the air strikes against Russia's Siberian weapons factory and on the city of Hamburg—all while being repaired at sea.

Five months had passed since then and at last the carrier's refurbishment was complete.

It had sailed with four squadrons of Americanized Su-34 VLR naval attack planes on board. An extremely dangerous aircraft, a single Su-34 could destroy up to ten enemy warplanes from up to a hundred miles away. It was also a highly capable dogfighter, and in close, it could rip up just about anything with its two nose-mounted cannons. But in reality, the Su-34 was a long range medium bomber. Its fuel capacity was so large, its two-man crew could fly fifteen hundred miles, drop more than 15,000 pounds of bombs, and fly back again—a three-thousand-mile combat radius, incredible for a midsize warplane.

The ship also carried three dozen Mi-24N helicopters, huge, cannon-heavy gunships, plus another dozen Ka-27 naval helicopters for antisub and search and rescue duties. Other assorted aircraft, including aerial refuelers and two C-2 AWACs planes, filled out the ship's air complement.

But the giant floating airbase was actually part battle-ship too. It was outfitted with four massive 18-inch gun batteries, two fore and two aft of the carrier's immense, ten-story superstructure. Cruise missile launchers dominated both sides of the ship's wide deck, weapons that could be quickly adapted to carry nuclear warheads. For its own protection, the ship also carried dozens of SAM launchers, rotary cannons, anti-ship missiles and CIWS Gatling guns.

Many of the ship's operations were run by computers—they took up most of the second deck. There were even some primitive robots on board to assist with things like loading shells or remotely operating the main deck elevator. The carrier's operations crew, the people who actually ran the ship, numbered just four hundred, instead of the more typical four thousand. This left space for more weapons, fuel, and airplanes.

The big ship was accompanied by an odd complement of escort vessels: two dozen armed tugboats. These workhorse vessels had been used previously to pull and push the huge ship before its engines were overhauled and put back on line.

Once the carrier was able to move on its own, the United Americans refurbished half the tugs by arming them with a variety of defensive weapons, including anti-ship, anti-aircraft and anti-submarine batteries. The others were outfitted as attack craft; they carried everything from Russian Z-guns, to Quad-50s and even a few mounted Gatling guns.

These little monsters could not only pack a punch, they moved surprisingly fast and maneuvered surprisingly well.

Everyone called them the Slugboats.

The USS *USA* was here to lead the United Americans' first-ever Pacific patrol.

It was a big step. America was still wild and wooly— and remained dangerous in some spots. But when the UA realized the AMC was leaving without a fight, they were suddenly faced with protecting two coastlines, two thousand miles apart.

From that perspective, and motivated by the trio of victories against the Russians, it just wouldn't be enough for the UA to let the AMC simply sail away and be taken at their word. They were bloodthirsty freaks most of them, and they'd desecrated a large part of the American southwest. The UA not only wanted them to leave; they wanted to make sure they never came back.

Tailing their evacuation ships all the way back to Asia was one way of pushing that message home.

But before this brave new mission commenced, a short ceremony was scheduled atop the LA City Hall near

Jim Cook's OP. Only a dozen people attended. Ten from the new, United American-sponsored armed force, simply christened the LA Army, and two were from the USS *USA*.

At exactly 0900 hours, this small group ran the American flag up the City Hall's flagpole—and at that moment, after almost countless years of war, hardship and spilled blood, the United States was officially free again. All the foreign occupiers—the Russians and their proxies, the AMC, the Mid-Aks, the Mongols, Vikings, Super-Nazis, Badlands freaks and many other circus-clown trouble-making groups in between—were gone. The Patriots had finally won.

Low-key for strategic reasons, the flag-raising was nevertheless the period at the end of the sentence at the end of a long chapter.

A new chapter was about to begin.

Chapter Four

Hawk Hunter did not attend the flag-raising ceremony.

He'd also missed the *USA*'s grand entrance into LA Harbor.

He'd been in his rack, inside his compartment, on the three-deck of the mammoth aircraft carrier, pillows over his head, asleep for both.

This was not like him, but this was how it was. The moment the huge ship passed into the Pacific via the canal, he'd swallowed four sleeping pills, locked the door to his cabin and forced himself to sleep. He'd finally succeeded but missed everything.

In one way, it seemed like the smart thing to do. He hadn't slept at all in the previous six days. From past Cuba to the western end of the canal, not a wink. Sleep deprivation could be a nasty thing, and when the body wants to shut down, it will.

But his 48-hour extended nap really didn't have to do with catching up on his rest. Just the opposite, he'd avoided going to sleep because he didn't want to dream.

He'd spent much of the time passing through the canal aloft. Piloting his refurbished F-16XL delta-winged superjet, he'd flown long hours, on hyper-alert, weaving back and forth twenty miles ahead of the carrier force, looking for any bad guys.

It was an important mission—but his spirit had been unsettled throughout. He would have thought just flying his old jet again would have been enough contentment to last him a lifetime, a dream he never dreamed of, never mind dreaming it would come true. Demolished on the deck of the very ship he was riding point for during the fight to wrest it from the Russians, his XL had been rebuilt by his friends in New York City as a gesture for helping free their metropolis from Moscow.

To be back in its cockpit, to be belted in again, everything as it had been—it was hard to believe.

Sometimes, things just happen.

But there was that other reason he'd stayed awake, the other reason for downing gallons of coffee, among other things. Because in the past half year, whenever he went to sleep and dreamed, which was almost every night, he saw flashes of a beautiful red-headed girl, wearing a plaid shirt, jeans and a white baseball hat. She'd been with him, in ways that he couldn't explain, since the absolutely crazy days following the strike on the Russian Siberian weapons factory. He'd seen her for real just three times in that month-long period—but had thought about her every day, almost every moment, since.

Who was she? What was she? He didn't know. Not yet, anyway. He'd done things in his life including passing over into parallel worlds—no mean feat.

But nothing had affected him like this.

Oddly, it wasn't the most unpleasant situation to be in. Not so far. But there was a high level of frustration to it, especially when it came to his dreams. Whenever she would appear to him, he would frequently try to ask her who she was, why she had this grip on him and what did it all mean. But as it was in dreams, something always interfered before she could reply, and he'd wake up a mess.

It was Freudian he was sure, but he knew the situation would carry over and affect his duties if he didn't do something about it.

So in the end he decided it was just better to stay awake.

The *USA* left Los Angeles at noon that day, going out with the tide. As with the flag raising ceremony, there was little fanfare.

It was a proud day, a solemn day. A day to be remembered. But there were no marching bands or water-gun flotillas, for the same reason the ceremony on the LA City Hall roof had been so subdued. When the UA won the Battle of New York City, they didn't just eject the Russians from America; they ended the era of the Kremlin using the Atlantic Ocean as its own private lake. These days, ships from the UA, Free Canada and many smaller allies sailed it freely.

This was not the case with the Pacific. The UA had zero intelligence on the vast ocean, no sightline beyond the horizon. Anything could be out there.

One of the first things discussed during the first meeting to put this mission together was the timing. Sure, the AMC was pulling out and America was whole again. But sailing into the Pacific might be like sailing into a black hole. So the consensus was: let's see what's out there before we have any parades.

The ship's departure did not go completely unrecognized, though. As it lifted anchor and was nudged out of the harbor by its dozen Slugboats, an honor guard made up of units from the new LA Army stood at attention on the dock nearby and saluted the monstrous ship as it passed.

It was a nice touch and so genuinely felt that the carrier radioed the CO of the honor guard with a message from the entire crew: "We'll have a parade when we get back."

An hour later, the carrier was steaming due west at more than 40 knots, an amazing speed for such a gargantuan ship. All systems were working. The Slugboats were in a phalanx position in front of her. Flights ops would begin within an hour.

From that moment on, the adventure would become real. Six months of training, planning, strategy sessions— all of it, now in the past.

Very soon, they were going to be way out there, all alone.

One hundred miles off the coast of Santa Monica, and thirty minutes prior to the first official flight ops, a briefing was called in the carrier's Surface Combat Information Center.

More readily known as the War Room, it was located on the One Deck just below the mammoth superstructure, a large enclosed space with lots of blinking lights and TV screens.

Though designed with typical Russian inattention to detail, this was the center of the UA's universe at the moment. Everything emanated from here.

The place was packed by the time Hunter arrived. Raised from his two days of enforced dream-free slumber, and yet still haunted by six months of dreams before that, he'd steeled himself for whatever was coming next.

He didn't look the same, though. He hadn't had a haircut in almost a year, and he let his beard grow to stubble these days before attacking it. He was thinner, quieter, and sometimes even had to talk to himself to keep from drifting off the matter at hand. He was different. His mental state was different.

He just hoped his friends wouldn't notice.

But of course they did.

Many of them were huddled around the war table when he walked in. Ben Wa, JT "Socket" Toomey, Captain Crunch, Rene Frost. The Cobra Brothers. The JAWS guys and NJ104 were also there. Sitting at the head of the table, illuminated by the planning board's fluorescent lights, was the man behind it all, everyone's best friend, Captain Bull Dozer.

He was the leader of the legendary merc group the 7th Calvary. He was also named mayor of New York City the day the Russians were driven out. Since then he'd become a wealthy man, a sudden fortune accumulated honestly. Putting his money to good use, he'd not only bankrolled this massive undertaking, but was its overall commander. This was fine with everyone else. Bull always dreamed big and always lived up to his nickname. For a mission like this, there was no one better to steer the ship.

Hunter took his seat at the table next to him. As the Air Ops commander, the Wingman was second-in-command of the patrol. A huge cup of black coffee in hand, he began emptying packets of sugar into it anxious for the briefing to begin. But he wasn't two sips in when he first heard about the mystery airplane over LA the night before.

Flying crazy, taunting the vanquished invaders, sowing confusion everywhere.

"It wasn't me," he blurted out.

Jim Cook reported what he and the JAWS guys had seen while the strange jet was overhead.

"From our combined notes, it sounds like it was a heavily modified Sukhoi Su-27," he began. "Russian-built fighter, old NATO codename, 'Flanker.' But it's actually related to the Su-34 fighters we fly now."

The Flanker looked like a slightly smaller cousin of the Su-34. A pure fighter, it was known for performing outrageous, nearly impossible, aerobatics at high speed and at frightening low altitudes. One maneuver was called the Cobra. The airplane would pull its nose straight up, coming to a sudden halt in mid-flight. This caused it to hang motionless for one, two, three seconds or more before finally falling back down to nose level and flying normally again.

The ability to do that in a dogfight, to slam on the brakes so your attacker overshoots you and winds up in your crosshairs, gave any pilot an incredible advantage.

Cook concluded: "What we saw most closely matched a Flanker. But who it belonged to, and what it was doing last night, I can't begin to guess."

Hunter added more sugar to his coffee. Another ghost to chase.

"If it flew out to sea then it could be carrier-based," he said, thinking out loud.

"So there's *another* flat top out there?" Ben said.

A universal groan went around the room. No one wanted to hear that.

Clancy Miller, the JAWS XO, spoke up: "I've got to say when I first saw its outline, I thought it was carrying some big-ass bombs under its wings. Now I think they might have been big-ass fuel tanks."

"Same here," his colleague, Mark Snyder, confirmed. "It could have been an ultra-long-range something."

Hunter threw two more packets of sugar into his coffee. "Either way," he said. "This trip just got a lot more interesting . . ."

There was a murmur of agreement. Everyone *just* knew that somewhere along the way, they were going to meet up with the mystery jet again.

This, Dozer understood.

"We concentrate on our main objective," he told the room. "But we must keep our eyes extra open for anything weird flying around out there."

The briefing got down to the nuts and bolts of the air ops. This was actually the start of a long day and night for the carrier. For the next eighteen hours, they would run around-the-clock CAP flights (for Combat Air Patrol, keeping watch on the ship from high above) plus hourly anti-submarine drills. Every flight squadron on the boat would be involved, including the helos.

It would be a tough-love test of the training they'd been doing for the past half year. If it didn't all work now, it probably never would.

It took about thirty minutes, but eventually all the air systems checks were approved. The carrier ops crew declared themselves ready. Robotics checked in, defensive weapons were good, the deck was clear, and the catapults were already leaking steam.

But as the assembled prepared to get up and go to work, Dozer stopped them.

"We have one more speaker," he said. He introduced the ship's meteorology officer, Commander Barry Keefe. Tall with movie star looks, he was known to everyone as Club, a nickname he'd picked up prewar when he was a cop in Boston.

The ship's pilots and crew followed Club's weather reports religiously; he'd worked wonders getting them through the Panama Canal, accurately predicting the weather in all of Central America for the entire time they were making the transit.

But it was unusual for him to address a briefing in the war room.

"A couple hours ago we finished calibrating our long range Doppler radar," he began, reading from notes. "We can expect calm seas and good flying weather for the next five days at least. That much I can assure you."

Those in the room gave him a short but humorous round of applause. Then many tried to get up a second time, only for Club to start again.

"But we've also discovered something else," he said loudly, making sure everyone was listening again. "By linking our Doppler with a few old weather satellites still in frequency, we found out that something on the other side of the Pacific is, at times, producing such vast amounts of radiation it's causing temperature spikes along the outer margins of the troposphere. We can actually measure these inverse fluctuations because they're coming all the way across the hemisphere and hitting us."

Those gathered would have thought all the jargon was a joke, except Club wasn't known for his joviality.

"One more time maybe, Commander?" Dozer requested.

Club gave them an edited version: "Somewhere out there, there's something that gets so bright and so hot it's heating up massive amounts of air around it to the point that it's affecting the weather in the South Pacific."

Those assembled finally got the message. There was dead silence for almost ten seconds.

"What the eff could it be?" Crunch finally asked.

The weatherman shrugged. "Something extremely powerful. When it flashes, it heats the atmosphere around it to the point where it will create a kind of manmade Aurora Borealis for a few seconds."

He paused for a moment then added: "It's a little piece of global warming, happening right before our eyes."

Chapter Five

Not only had Hunter's XL been rebuilt and refitted, its undercarriage had been reinforced so it could do the carrier's catapult shots and trap landings. The *USA* was unique in that its planes could take off via catapult or the ship's ski-jump bow. Routine launches went off the jump, to save fuel. But if you wanted to get airborne fast, the side-deck catapult was the way to go.

Hunter would be the first off the deck once the CAP launches began, ready to take up his usual position on point. Ben and JT ran two squadrons of Su-34s; their airplanes would quickly follow, getting airborne and setting up an aerial screen above the carrier group as it plowed westward. Those squadrons run by Crunch and Frost would be on ready-reserve, ready to scramble.

A dozen of the navalized Hind helicopters and six of the Ka-27s would also take off; the Cobra Brothers were co-COs of the rotary units. The huge Hinds were in charge of close-in protection; the half dozen Ka-27s would be doing combined ops training with a like number of Slugboats.

This was the schedule. Similar operations would launch again at 1600 hours, with Frost and Crunch replacing Ben and JT's squadrons. Once night fell, they'd do it all over again—two more times—Hunter flying point man for it all.

If everything went as they hoped, when the sun rose the following day, the tail end of the AMC evacuation fleet should be in sight.

Once the briefing finished, Hunter headed straight for the Ready Room to get suited up. He found an unexpected visitor waiting for him.

It was Anthony Antonio Antonioni, better known as Tony 3. A jovial bowling ball of a man, he was a filmmaker who had worked with Hunter and the UA in the past. Bull Dozer had hired him to document the USS *USA*'s first foray into the Pacific.

But Tony did not work small. While his shoulder-mounted video camera provided much of his footage, he'd also installed a dozen stationary cameras around the flight deck to catch the best of the carrier's launch and recovery operations. He'd also wired the deck with more than two dozen microphones, capturing sounds he planned to include in the movie's soundtrack, working title: "Pride of the USA."

Hunter had helped Tony with his wiring during free moments transiting Panama Canal. That's why the filmmaker had come to talk to him. He looked troubled.

"I felt I had to tell you first," Tony began. "Something very strange is going on with my sound equipment."

Hunter started to climb into his flight suit. "Did I screw up the wiring?" he asked.

Tony shook his head. "Hardly. No, it's something I'm picking up on my recorders. An unwanted ambient sound. The weird thing is it's not coming from the carrier itself—it's coming from, like all around us."

"What's it sound like?"

Tony shrugged. "Deep, vibrating. But when you slow it down, it sounds like a million bees, all buzzing at once."

"And it's coming from . . . everywhere?"

"It's in the background of all my audio tapes."

Hunter stopped suiting up for a moment. "What could it be?"

Tony just shrugged again. He was usually brimming with enthusiasm and good cheer. But not at the moment.

"I've never heard it before," he said. "But I've never been aboard a mile-long aircraft carrier at sea before either. All I know is I'm hearing something out there."

Hunter resumed putting on his flight gear; the helmet was always last.

"Okay, please brief Bull about it," he told Tony. "Maybe the ship ops guys will know what it is. In any case, he'll be thrilled to learn we've got another mystery on our hands."

Hunter checked the time. Two minutes before his launch.

Tony asked him: "How are you set for vitamins?"

It wasn't just coffee alone that had kept him awake those six days. Tony had a special kind of medication that helped.

"Long hours ahead," Hunter replied.

The next thing he knew, he had a bottle of small green pills in his hand.

"Got to stay awake," Tony told him. "Especially these days."

Chapter Six

Hunter's launch went smoothly, the ship's powerful catapult flinging the XL off the side deck at 120 mph in two seconds.

He put the superjet on its tail and went straight up to 40,000 feet. Turning over in one long graceful arc, his nose pointed west, he began to scan the skies all around him.

He knew that just over the horizon, from this height several hundred miles away, the retreating AMC ships were chugging along, heading to someplace in Asia. Once on their tails, the UA fleet would shadow them until every last one of them disembarked, cementing the message that they should never set foot in America again.

He drew a deep breath of oxygen, trying to appreciate what had happened here. He'd fought for years to rid America of foreign invaders, of enemies of any kind. So did all his friends. But deep down, he never really thought it would come true.

But here he was.

The country was free, his plane was fixed, and thanks to Tony 3, he was *really* flying.

*****

Everything went well that morning and afternoon, and through the double-decker night ops as well.

Hunter flew every shift, buoyed in between by endless cups of black coffee containing endless spoonful's of sugar and a green pill or two mixed in. And anytime he found himself succumbing to a distracting notion—like beautiful angels in white baseball caps—he willed himself to put it out of his mind and concentrate on other things, the more pleasant the better.

He thought about his girlfriend Sara, back in Sherbrook, Free Canada. Cute, blonde, sensuous, funny—his only complaint was that they weren't together enough. They were both in the special ops biz and time apart was just another occupational hazard.

He thought of his long-time ex-girlfriend Dominique. Off the charts gorgeous, in a regal kind of way, she was presently with Mike Fitzgerald on the Ohio-class submarine USS *Fitz*, watching over the Atlantic while the USS *USA* patrolled the Pacific.

He even thought of Viktoria Robotov. Though she was the daughter of his arch enemy Viktor Robotov, she'd nevertheless turned him into a puddle of goo when they'd met recently, so captivating were her dark, smoldering good looks.

All this fantasizing helped pass the time and his special blend of java kept him wide awake and alert.

The formula worked so well, by the midway point of his double night op, he'd decided he never wanted to go to sleep again.

It was now 0500 hours; dawn was just minutes away.

For the fifth time in 24 hours, Hunter pulled on his flight suit, drank his coffee, popped his pill, then made his way up to the flight deck and strapped into the XL.

He was being lined up on the side catapult when his body began buzzing—and it wasn't just from Tony's vitamins this time. His internal warning system was lighting up; a message from the cosmos was coming in. It always arrived as a feeling, and at the moment, it was telling him something big was going to happen soon and he should be ready for it.

He placed so much faith in these messages from beyond that he made a quick call to the carrier's air combat room and requested that all four squadrons of Su-34s be launched immediately instead of the usual two for two staggered ops. All helos should get airborne, too, and the entire ship should be put at battle stations.

The requests went directly to Bull Dozer, who officially made them so.

Hunter launched a half minute later. Flung out over the water, hitting 120 knots in two seconds, he lit his afterburner and steered west. His body never stopped vibrating; his senses felt like they were in the strato-sphere. Adrenalin was flooding through his body, adding to the high. He was ready for anything.

Staying low this time, he was rocketing along above the waves at barely 250 feet. A morning mist had covered the ocean's surface, typical in this part of the Pacific. But he stayed true to this course for thirty seconds—and when he broke out of the fog, before him was the ass end of the giant AMC evacuation fleet, just going over the horizon.

Thirty-six vessels in all, most were elderly passenger liners pressed into service, an old Russian trick. Moving at about 15 knots, they were now sailing in a closed-box formation, six lines of six. The entire fleet did not take up more than half a square mile.

Hunter roared over them, still very low, still on after-burner, waking up anyone who wasn't awake already. His sonic boom was so powerful, it bounced off the top of the ocean itself, creating huge waves which further battered the retreating ships.

This was intentional cruelty. He would never have attempted any radio communications with the AMC ships; he'd much rather blow their eardrums out. The AMC wasn't a real army, they were not professional soldiers. They were thugs, murderers, rapists and psycho-paths—and he had less than zero respect for them.

He wanted them to know he was up here and that an entire UA battle fleet was now behind them, watching their every move.

At just about the same time Hunter was buzzing the AMC fleet, Slugboat 7 had just arrived at a position known as flank south one.

It was twenty miles out and ten miles ahead of the USS *USA*, sealing the southern edge. This was picket duty, making sure something coming from this direction didn't surprise the battle group.

Lieutenant Jayden Ruggeri was the boat's CO.

All was well in his patrol area. He could see the AMC ships out on the horizon. He had a clear channel of communications back to the carrier. And just as Club had predicted, the skies were clear, and the sea was calm.

Until . . .

The heavily armed tug was moving at 25 knots when a sudden shudder shook the vessel bow to stern. They'd hit something in the water.

Ruggeri immediately cut engines and came to a stop. He was quickly down on the deck and, with the help of three crewmen, hauled the mangled object on board.

It looked like a miniature airplane. About five feet long, with a wingspan to match, it was built of thin aluminum, had a small engine and propeller. It was also carrying two bombs under its wings. A simple but not crude design, it had crashed into the water somehow, colliding with the Slugboat's heavily padded bow.

Once secured on the deck, the Slugboat crew surrounded it, never seeing anything quite like it.

Finally, one crewman asked Ruggeri: "Is this what they call a drone, sir?"

The words weren't out of his mouth when Ruggeri looked up to see the sky was suddenly filled with these things. Way up high, *hundreds* of the propeller-powered drones, flying in six separate swarms, all in perfect chevron formations.

Ruggeri quickly hit the Slugboat's warning klaxon; it began blaring, calling the crew to battle stations.

When he looked up again, he saw the swarm was turning right for the carrier.

Hunter spotted the drones just a few seconds before the Slugboat crew—but he'd heard them just a few seconds before that.

Like a million bees. Making a sound that was coming from all directions.

He'd seen a number of top-secret drone flight tests before the Big War. They never involved more than two or three of the mini airplanes at a time. Now, he was looking at three hundred or more unmanned aerial vehicles, coming out of the south, flying at 10,000 feet.

Yet when he looked down at his radar screen, he saw . . . nothing.

"That's not good," he said aloud.

The wisdom of launching all four squadrons was now evident because something very alarming was happening here. There were hundreds of these things—and none of them were showing up on radar.

Stealth? That was something Hunter had only heard whispers about before the war started—at least in this universe. Military aircraft flying around but not getting picked up on radar. The idea was frightening on many levels, especially to a fighter pilot. Radar was your eyes up here. If the other side wasn't playing the same game, then it would be like dogfighting a ghost.

It got worse. As the swarm drew closer, Hunter could see many of the drones were carrying a pair of bombs under their wings; he was sure they were 150-lb high-explosive shells. Times two, then times at least three hundred, meant almost 100,000 pounds of explosives, or nearly fifty *tons* of highly flammable bombs were coming at the carrier.

It was more than enough to sink the USS *USA*.

But the big ship was not the swarm's target.

The four alert squadrons were airborne and were getting in position behind Hunter's XL, ready to intercept the UAVs. But suddenly the first chevron of drones started falling out of the sky—and they weren't aiming for the carrier or the Slugboats.

Incredibly, the drones began slamming into the AMC ships. Like kamikazes, they were sacrificing themselves but in a highly coordinated fashion. Five drones per troopship, three quarters of a ton of bombs exploding on each one. The passenger ships were old and un-armored. Fifteen hundred pounds of bombs was more than enough to cripple them, if not sink them outright.

The attack was methodical, mechanized—and brutal. No sooner had the first wave of drones hit, when the second wave began descending too. The combined scream of the little aircraft spiraling out of the sky was deafening. The explosions sounded like syncopated cannon fire. Spirals of flame shot into the air. Gushes of smoke and water flew hundreds of feet high. In seconds, a dozen of the AMC ships were sinking and another dozen were aflame.

It was at that moment the vanguard of airplanes from the USS *USA* arrived on the scene; formed up and coming out of the east, Hunter's XL was in the lead. The drones were traveling at about 250 knots—the UA jets were much faster and infinitely better armored. But no sooner had Hunter and the others turned into the swarm, when, like magic, the last line of drones suddenly reversed course and began steering right for the oncoming fighter jets.

The two groups merged seconds later, and it was instant pandemonium. Not only did the drones not show up on radar, the American pilots weren't able to get in position to fire on them because the UAVs were using the same tactic as when attacking the AMC fleet. Kamikaze, hari-kari, aerial seppuku—whatever you wanted to call it, the drones were intent on sacrificing themselves, and their bomb loads, to bring down the UA jets.

It was pure self-preservation that caused the UA pilots to quickly break off the engagement, climb like hell and get out of the dangerous furball. It was all over in a matter of seconds. The drones presented themselves as such aerial hazards, the Americans had no choice but to turn away.

Once this happened, this last wave of drones regrouped, turned and fell as one onto the burning AMC fleet.

Hunter watched it all from 10,000 feet, so stunned his hands could barely feel the controls. The sudden and bizarre attack on the AMC fleet was bad enough. But something else had happened here: for the first time, his superior fighter pilot skills had done him no good.

He'd once shot down a hundred Russian airplanes in a massive, almost mythical, dogfight. He'd shot down hundreds more enemy aircraft since.

But even he couldn't stop something like this.

Small, cheap aerial machines designed to do just one thing—martyr themselves to destroy a target. A swarm of them would be almost impossible to stop under any conditions.

And . . . if that were the case, if this was the dark future of the world—then his greatest fear of all might be coming true.

The day of the fighter pilot might be near its end.

Chapter Seven

The USS *USA* had gone dead in the water.

Klaxons were blaring, trouble lights were spinning, and all hands were at their battle stations. All the Slug-boats had sprinted back to the carrier and had formed a tight protective ring around her, some at rest, some orbiting one hundred yards out. Four Su-34s from JT's squadron were also flying continuous rings around the ship, keeping an eye on the skies, while others dealt with what was happening below.

A scene of unimaginable horror was being played out not five hundred feet off the carrier's bow. Thousands of AMC soldiers were dying right before their eyes. Many were drowning; others were succumbing to wounds suffered in the massive drone attack fifteen minutes before. But most were being eaten by sharks. Lured by the scent of blood in the water, hundreds of them had raced to the scene. With tens of thousands of bodies floating everywhere, and thousands more helpless and in the water, it soon turned into a ghastly feeding frenzy.

An emergency briefing had been called in the War Room, and, on landing, all the principal air personnel hurried there. Two of Tony 3's video cameras, set up on the nose of the carrier, had chronicled the entire attack on the AMC fleet. Now they continued to record the gut-wrenching savagery going on very close to the massive warship.

Jammed into the room, everyone was standing, all eyes transfixed on the large video screen showing Tony's twin camera feeds, dumbstruck by the carnage, live and in color. It was so gruesome, many had to turn away.

At the head of the planning table was Captain Bull Dozer. He looked ashen, his facial features distorted into a grimace of shock.

What had they sailed into here?

He finally broke the silence.

"They always say 'my enemy's enemy is my friend,'" he said. "But at the moment, I'm not sure."

"Do we really want to be friends with someone who's responsible for something like this?" Ben asked, finally turning away from the screen himself. "I mean the AMC are the scum of the earth. But . . ."

He let his voice trail off.

"But there's got to be a reason why the drones chose not to hit us," JT said. "The AMC was retreating, going home. Whoever did this must have known that, right?"

"I don't think anyone is helping us," Hunter said, speaking for the first time. "I think someone is showing us something. Showing us what they can do."

"Sending a message," Frost said.

"Then it came through loud and clear," Crunch said. "Whatever we can do to the AMC, we can do to you, too."

Dozer squeezed his eyes sockets, as if the added pressure to his cranium would help him make a very difficult decision.

The question was, what should they do now?

Watch thousands of people drown, watch thousands more being eaten—and just stand by and do nothing? Should they sail away? Or should the UA put themselves in harm's way and try to save the lives of thousands of murderers and rapists?

"We're still human beings," Dozer finally half-whispered. "And so are they."

He paused another moment, rubbed his eyes again, and then said: "We've got to try to help them . . ."

The deck of the USS *USA* suddenly came back to life.

Crew chiefs, refuelers, armorers, cat men, pilots. Lots of rushing around, all of it with a purpose.

A dozen fresh Su-34s were brought on deck and made ready to launch. In front of them, already hooked up to the side catapult, was Hunter's crazily bulked-up XL.

This was not going to be a regular air op. This was a mercy mission of gigantic proportions. And of all the sea trials and training the carrier's crew had undergone before starting this voyage, this was the one mission they'd not planned for. Search and rescue, man overboard, aircraft crash at sea—they'd drilled endlessly for those things. But the idea that they might need to rescue thousands of people from the water just never occurred to them. Yet here they were, about to do it anyway.

As was usually the case with the UA, it was a plan on the fly. Launch all the helicopters and send out all the Slugboats and between them retrieve as many souls as possible without the crews falling prey to the sharks. In the meantime, the dozen Su-34s would launch and replace the six current CAP flights which were getting low on fuel and needed to trap back on the boat.

Once airborne, Hunter would try to wrangle it all, looking down from 5,000 feet. But they weren't kidding themselves. Carrier launches had been compared to ballets at sea—and the orchestration to make one work was immense. But no amount of aeronautical expertise was going to change the fact that this was an impossible undertaking from the start.

There had been more than 120,000 AMC troops aboard the thirty-six ships, not counting their supremely unlucky crews. All but five of the evacuation fleet had sunk by now; thirty-one were in pieces or at the bottom of the sea. Those still afloat were in various stages of sinking, and all of them were aflame.

By this time, some of the survivors from the other ships had managed to make their way through the sharks and over to these five vessels which were clustered near the rear of the devastated column. They were now either clambering to get aboard them or clinging to debris in the waters around them. But this was also where lots of the victims of the drone strike were floating. The water was so bloody it was red, attracting even more sharks to the area.

Still, the UA rescue force had to concentrate its efforts here. Have the helos and the Slugboats keep picking up as many survivors as possible, until . . . when? The deck was packed? So much so, aircraft won't be able to land? Or do they put thousands of their dreaded enemy below decks?

That was just the beginning of the problem. If the thought of bringing thousands of AMC warriors aboard the carrier was not a pleasant one, what was the UA going to do with them once they were here? Nurse them back to health so they could drop them off to rape, murder and pillage somewhere else?

What the UA was trying to do didn't make sense—except for one thing. They were Americans.

It was just not in them to sit by and do nothing.

*****

49

Hunter was tied in, ready to go.

One last check of his RPMs, then the catapult officer flashed him his steam pressure number. Everything jived. He needed only to salute the deck officer and he'd be thrown off the ship at 120 mph with a lot of the ship's war company to follow, unintentional players in a rescue mission from hell.

Hunter put his hand up to his helmet's bill, ready to give the launch salute. The deck officer was crouched in his set-go position. The catapult steam was billowing and mixing with the swirls of smoke. A dozen navalized Hind helicopters were nearby, waiting to get airborne. The half dozen Ka-27s were behind them, waiting to do the same thing.

Hunter's fingers touched his helmet's sun visor . . . and stayed there.

Because suddenly his body was vibrating again.

Top to bottom and back again, as always, the *feeling* engulfed him. And it was giving one clear message this time: Don't move. Don't launch. Stay in place.

All eyes were suddenly on him—and he had to admit it was an odd time to hesitate. Still he called the carrier's air control room and spoke directly to Bull.

He simply said: "Let's hang on a moment . . ."

An instant later, the air around them began buzzing again. All those eyes suddenly went to the southwest.

Looking so much like a storm of locusts, another drone swarm was coming their way.

But still, Hunter did not move.

He held his salute, and everything just remained frozen.

They waited ten long seconds, just on his feeling alone. But as before, at the very last moment, the swarm turned away—and began falling on the survivors of the first horrible attack.

Once more, the ocean was rocked by explosions as the kamikaze drones slammed into the five remaining AMC troopships. Three went down immediately, with all hands and anyone in the water nearby.

The final two ships stayed afloat, but just a minute longer. Then both capsized and went down too, smoking in flames—many more hundreds sucked down with them.

Watching it all from the carrier, to the ship's crew, this was almost as ghastly as the first attack.

But then came an even more morbid twist.

It was like a switch was suddenly thrown somewhere. Although the last of the AMC ships had gone to the bottom, there were still many hundreds of AMC soldiers in the water—with nowhere to go. So, the last two waves of drones broke formation and began flying very low across the waves. These UAVs were not carrying bombs; they were armed with small machine guns and they began picking off the helpless survivors. Zipping back and forth, like giant bloodthirsty insects, emitting that disturbing buzzing sound, it was a sick triumph of simple but effective technology.

It lasted about five minutes, just about everyone on the carrier watched in silent horror as the drones finished off the last of the AMC soldiers, leaving their remains as chum for the sharks.

And finally, it was over. No more desperate cries were picked up on Tony's microphones; no more people thrashing about in the bloody red water.

The slaughter was complete.

There was silence for almost a minute. The sea became calm and the wind died down. The last of the sniper drones, about fifty in all, climbed as one. Slotting into an arrow formation, they turned west and started to fly away.

Only then did Hunter complete his salute.

"Good for launch," he said.

Chapter Eight

Two seconds later, the XL was out over the water and spiraling to 40,000 feet.

Hunter had punched his radio receive button on the way up and was soon talking to Dozer.

"Hey, Hawk," Bull began. "What are you doing?"

"Following them," Hunter replied. "Following the swarm."

"Will you have enough gas to do that?"

"I'm tanked up . . ."

"But who knows how far these guys have flown?" Dozer asked him. "Or where they're going?"

"We don't," Hunter said. "But they don't show up on radar, so if we lose visual on them now, we might not have another chance. And who really knows? We *might* be next."

Dozer was learning real fast what it was like to be the commander of a ship, a crash course if there ever was one. He'd been CO of the 7th Cavalry merc group for many years, so he had management skills. And he was mayor of New York City, so he had people skills. But he also believed in fate and luck. Fate had saved them from the mercy mission from hell. All the copters had stood down, the CAP squadron was getting launched and the

Slugboats had resumed their defensive ring around the carrier. And by some mysterious good luck, he supposed, the USS *USA* went untouched while the murderous drone massacre happened not 500 feet away.

The question was, should they count their blessings and for the sake of ship and crew, get the message, and learn to peacefully co-exist with this giant vicious unknown on the other side of the Pacific?

Or should they go find out who the hell they were?

If anyone could track down the source of the drone swarm, it was Hunter—this Dozer knew. That was the conundrum. His friend had a bad habit of going off solo on extremely hazardous missions—and getting lost. Sometimes for days, sometimes for years.

Dozer felt it was his duty to avoid that. No matter what the UA did, it always revolved around the Wingman. He was their superstar, their superhero. To risk losing him again, now . . . for this?

But then there was the other half of the argument and it was the same reason they'd mounted the short-circuited rescue mission: they were Americans. If there was something evil out here, it was in their DNA to go find it and try to stop it.

It's what they did.

Dozer was silent for a few moments, but finally relented.

"OK, you win," he told Hunter. "Just keep in touch—and for Christ's sake, don't get lost again."

But Hunter barely heard him.

He'd turned the XL west and increased speed. Inside a minute, he'd spotted the tail end of the drone swarm way off in the distance. They were at about 25,000 feet, had increased speed to 300 knots, and had further tightened up their arrow formation.

He noted his position: the California coast was now 1,200 miles behind him. Nearest piece of land going west? Hawaii—more than 1,000 miles away.

But the swarm wasn't heading in either direction. It was flying southwest—where there really was nothing, for thousands and thousands of miles.

So, where the hell were they going?

Hunter knew enough fuel-saving tricks to extend the XL's range to about 2,200 miles. After that, it would get dicey. But he had no other choice than to stay glued to the UAVs and see where they led.

He rose to 45-Angels, took a little green pill, and settled in.

He knew this was going to take a while.

Dozens of thoughts were soon buzzing around his head.

But one eventually won out: Whoever built these drones possessed some extremely sophisticated technology for the post-Big War world. While there were plenty of high-tech weapons around—warplanes, warships, tanks, helicopters and more—the path to *higher* technologies had been pretty much blocked since the war. That's why customized weapons abounded, his XL superjet being the perfect example.

But the drone swarm was actually low-tech masquerading as high-tech, and doing so quite effectively. Hundreds of inexpensive, heavily armed, incredibly dangerous, unmanned flying kamikazes that didn't show up on radar? This was a game changer and, caught in an endless loop, what it really meant kept coming around to hit Hunter in the gut.

If the best fighter pilot in the world couldn't defeat these things, then what good was he?

Two hours passed.

He stayed at 45,000 feet; the swarm stayed four miles below and about five miles ahead of him. They'd continued flying southwest, never diverting from their course, never going over 300 knots.

Sometimes he had to fly a few, slight zigzags so he wouldn't overtake them, but at least he wasn't burning up his fuel in some kind of high-speed chase. The drones weren't in any hurry to get anywhere, and so neither was he.

He was flying in dead radio silence . . . almost. He was certain the drones didn't have any radar capability, so they weren't going to spot him tailing them. But he wanted to stay off the radio too so as not to give even a single clue that he was looking down at them from four miles up.

So the way he stayed in touch with the carrier was through mic-pops. He would hold down his radio button for exactly two seconds. The pop of static would be picked up back on the ship, answered with two similar pops and then triangulated with other known points, giving them Hunter's general location.

But the farther he got away from the carrier the fainter these mic-pops would become, until, at least in theory, they would get too weak to hear and disappeared altogether.

At the moment, he was sending a pop every fifteen minutes, and the carrier would pop in return. He hoped they knew approximately where he was.

Because he sure didn't.

Chapter Nine

The hours passed slowly. Two hours turned into three, then four, then five . . . then six.

Hunter was now 1,800 miles and four green pills southwest of the carrier. Still he saw nothing but the deep blue Pacific below. And with each exchange of mic-pops, the responses grew even weaker.

As the sixth hour passed into the seventh, his red fuel-warning light began slowly pulsating. He'd crossed his bingo point a long time ago, meaning he no longer had enough gas to return to the carrier unaided. For the last hour, he'd been feathering the XL's big engine, gliding for miles at some points. He'd also employed some power-reduction systems inside the superjet's turbine, again to use as little gas as possible.

But now his flat-panel fuel gauge was sliding to the bottom of the red zone and the warning light was blinking with more urgency. He watched it almost hypnotized for a few seconds. Though it was not the first time he'd experienced this gloomy feeling, the blinking light confirmed it: this was probably going to be a one-way mission.

But then a moment after that . . . his body began buzzing again.

This particular feeling was very familiar and distinct. It was his internal radar telling him there was another aircraft nearby. A real aircraft—not some drone. And judging by the intensity of the vibe, it was a big one.

It took him the next few moments to clear some cloud cover . . . but then he saw it.

It was flying at 35,000 feet, three miles down range and about two miles below him. But it was not just some gigantic airplane. It was a Boeing 747 jumbo jet—with another 747 attached to it. Two enormous fuselages, two enormous tails, and a 500-foot common wing with six outlying jet engines attached. It was to aeronautics what the USS *USA* was to warships: simply gargantuan.

He began slowly descending towards the flying monster, hoping if it had radar, he was still in a blind spot. The huge plane was moving at barely 200 knots—almost a dangerously slow speed. But there was a reason for it: the flock of sniper drones had slowed down and slotted in behind it and was now following it. It was a bizarre scene. The hybrid plane looked like a huge mechanical bird leading dozens of younger ones through the scattered clouds above the blue, late afternoon Pacific.

Hunter turned his radio to all channels, its scanning feature set to stop at the strongest signal nearest to him. One assaulted his headphones almost immediately. It was coming from the huge airplane and it sounded very strange: like one, very loud, echoing *bloop!*

As soon as he'd heard it, the big plane adjusted its course slightly, turning a bit more to the south. The flock responded in kind.

He realized what was going on. The weird noise was a transmission burst—hundreds of radio signals compressed into one odd-sounding rush of electronic noise that could be interpreted by a specialized receiver. Old fashioned radio commands. That was how the flying monster communicated with its deadly flock.

It was a fantastic discovery—and a mind-boggling use of postwar technology. But it was mostly lost on Hunter because he couldn't take his eyes off his fuel gauge. It was getting so low he knew he wouldn't be able follow the huge mothership and its drones for more than ten minutes, if that.

He looked grimly to the vast open ocean below, knowing he would have to ditch down there soon. Sara. Dominique. Viktoria . . . he thought of them all, whispered each of their names three times. It was then that the reality of the situation really gripped him.

This was going to be a shitty way to die.

But then, another miracle of sorts: His body began buzzing again and this time it felt like a bolt of electricity running through him. He focused back on the giant airplane just in time to see three more aircraft maneuvering in front of it.

These planes were nowhere as large as the Jumbo-Jumbo, but were still substantially sized. As he got closer, he saw they were old Boeing 707 jet liners that had been converted into aerial refuelers like the KC-135. He also knew these guys were air mercs; their garish plane art and crazy-bright circus colors gave them away.

As his own fuel gauge started to blink yellow, telling him he was almost dry, the trio of planes lined up in a three-across flight pattern and unreeled their fuel hoses. The Jumbo-Jumbo rose up to meet them and with admirable piloting, managed to quickly hook onto all three.

It took almost another five minutes to fill what had to be enormous fuel tanks on the big plane. But just as the tankers were finishing, two smaller but longer fuel hoses started reeling out of the back of the Jumbo-Jumbo.

Incredibly, one by one, the sniper drones lined up on these hoses and started getting refueled themselves. Again, Hunter was astonished by the aerial technology on display.

While the sniper drones continued their aerial gas-up, the three merc tankers finally broke off and headed their separate ways.

Hunter looked down at his fuel gauge again and felt his heart drop to his boots. He had two minutes' worth of gas left.

After that, he was going into the drink.

Chapter Ten

Night had fallen aboard the USS *USA*.

Flight ops continued, there were twelve CAP planes in the air at all times protecting the carrier fifty miles out in all directions.

The Slugboats maintained their defensive ring around the big ship, their gun crews on high alert, ready for anything. The Ka-27s were also flying, looking over the Slugboats from above.

Bull Dozer was in the War Room, sitting at his planning table, an unlit cigar butt clenched in his teeth. A little red, white and blue wooden airplane was the only piece on the lighted board. It was positioned about 1500 miles from the carrier's present location.

This represented the last mic-pop they'd received from Hunter. They'd been exchanging the secret signals every fifteen minutes, but Hunter hadn't been heard from in more than an hour.

Dozer finally threw the cigar butt away and put his head down on the table. He hadn't slept in two days and it had been a grueling forty-eight hours to be awake. First the two hellish drone attacks and then letting Hunter go off on his own, chasing the UAVs with no idea where he would end up.

The carrier was heading southwest, its course as close as they could come to reaching Hunter's last known position, burning it out at almost 45 knots. But Dozer could do the math. The XL was a fantastic airplane, but as Hunter himself often said, it didn't run on pixie dust. Even by the most optimistic estimates, the Wingman was probably running out of gas at that very moment.

Crunch appeared in the War Room, carrying a huge cup of coffee for Dozer. The lights in the room were dim, better to see the various glow boards and maps. But it also added to the deep sense of gloom inside.

"Nothing yet, I assume," he asked Dozer. The ship's CO could barely keep his eyes open. He just shook his head slowly.

Crunch passed him the coffee and asked, "Did you see the medics report about the stiff in the basement?"

Dozer shook his head no. In the aftermath of the second drone attack on the AMC fleet, one of the victims' bodies became entangled in the ship's anchor chain and wound up being hauled onboard. Instead of dumping it over the side, the carrier's medical team asked to examine it first, just to determine what kind of shape the AMC warriors were in when they abandoned LA. It was purely an intelligence-gathering effort; know thine enemy even though in this case, there probably weren't many of them left.

"This guy must have been living the high life in LA," Crunch told him. "Well-fed, uniform in good shape. Boots looked new."

But Dozer had gone back to staring at his planning board. He looked beyond exhausted.

Crunch told him, "If you want to hit the rack, Bull, I'll be glad to stand watch here."

Dozer didn't reply. Instead he drained the huge mug of hot black coffee in a series of giant gulps. It was gone in seconds.

"If I leave now," he finally told Crunch, "I'll feel like I'm giving up on him." He paused a few moments and then added: "I should never have let him go."

Crunch took a seat across the table from him. He was beat too. They all were.

"All that would have done was put Hawk in a position to disobey your orders," he told Dozer. "He would have gone anyway."

Dozer drained the last few drops from his cup, and then he looked up at him.

"What the hell are we doing out here, Crunchie?" he asked solemnly. "We got this big boat and all these airplanes, and we decide to come out here and start swinging our dicks around? Well, pride comes before a fall. And here we are."

Crunch almost laughed. "That's one way of looking at it. Another way would be to say we are protecting our left coast. We're a country again. We would have been derelict in our duties if we didn't attempt to secure what has been returned to us."

Dozer just shook his head. "A noble mistake, then?"

"It's not over until it's over," Crunch replied, adding, "But as captain, I guess it's up to you to determine just when that will be."

Dozer looked back at the planning table and the little wooden airplane.

"I got a real bad feeling about this one," he said, his voice barely above a whisper now. "I know he's been lost before. And he was gone for all those years, just where he didn't even know. But this time? I just don't know. We might have killed the greatest hero America has ever seen."

He tried a mic-pop again—they waited in silence for a minute, but there was no reply.

"I knew I could never be him," Dozer said suddenly. "But damn I've tried so hard to be like him."

He studied the map of the Pacific once more, then added: "But I have this ship and everyone on it to think about as well."

He put his finger atop the little wooden airplane.

"We'll sail to this point," he said. "And if we can't find anything, then we'll have to seriously consider turning around and going home."

Chapter Eleven

Joso Gabang had been in the aerial refueling business since the end of World War III.

He and his younger brothers, Kadir and Omo, had bought the old 707 right after the hostilities had ceased and air mercs were suddenly in demand around the world. The Gabang Brothers' realized early that the safe money was not so much in being a mercenary combat pilot, but in selling fuel to them.

It had been a wise decision—and a profitable one. Reliability was a rare commodity in the postwar world; a good street rep was needed. Because they took great pains to be on time and in the right place for their customers to fuel up, the brothers were usually able to get their money in advance. Someday they hoped to own a fleet of tankers.

One of their biggest clients was the double-hulled 747 they'd just refueled. It was so enormous, it took their plane and two other independent contractors to fill its tanks. They didn't know who the customer was, not exactly. But anytime they took their payment—in pure silver, the world's currency these days—the bag always arrived with a tiny yellow star stamped on it.

Nothing else—just that single yellow star.

Their part of the refueling triad complete, the Gabang's 707 turned west and headed for its next hook-up: a squadron of vintage F-105s fighter-bombers found in the jungles of Vietnam and rebuilt into a free-lance ground-attack group. They were presently 400 miles to the northwest, on their way to a mission near Honolulu. After that, the Gabang boys could head back home to their base on the Marshall Islands, about 1,500 miles away.

Joso was the plane's pilot; his brothers were the hose men. Their job was to reel out the long flexible aerial pipe and hook it onto the customer's refueling probe. It took some expertise, but they were good at it by now.

Joso's mission was to keep them flying, but with the automatic pilot engaged, he usually had a lot of downtime between fill-ups. While his brothers were pushing around the hoses and getting the pumps reprimed for the next customer, Joso was usually taking a nap.

He was in the midst of setting up his ruck sack turned pillow, when his headphones suddenly crackled to life. It was his brother, Omo, calling from the back of the airplane.

All he said was: "Get back here now!"

Joso scrambled to the rear of the craft to find an extremely confusing situation.

Looking out the tiny, rear-facing refueling window, he could see a jet fighter flying no more than fifty feet off their tail. At first Joso thought it was a merc pilot who'd mistaken their 707 for another tanker. (This was hard to do though; the Gabang plane was painted in bright yellow and pink, all the easier for their paying customers to spot them from far away.)

But in the next second, Joso realized this was no ordinary jet fighter. This thing was delta-shaped, highly tricked out, painted red, white and blue and seemed to come from some science fiction author's imagination.

There was only one airplane like this in the world. It was an F-16XL. And only one person in the world flew it: The Wingman.

"It looks like he's trying to tell us something," his other brother Kadir whispered to him, his voice trembling.

Joso started shaking too; he'd heard about the famous Hawk Hunter, but never in a million years did he think he'd ever see him in the flesh. Yet now, here he was—and he was gesturing to him.

Joso climbed down into the small refueling cockpit to get a better look. Once he knew he had Joso's attention, the pilot first pointed to the six-pack of Vulcan cannons poking out of the XL's nose. Then he made a cross with two of his fingers . . . and then pointed directly at Joso.

That's when it came together for the eldest Gabang brother.

To use an old American term: this was a stick-up.

PART TWO

Battle of the Wingmen

Chapter Twelve

The mid-air robbery took two minutes.

As soon as his fuel gauges reached the top of the green zone again, Hunter gave the Gabang boys the wave off and disconnected from their fuel nozzle.

He put the XL into a screaming left bank and went into a dive. He was breathing normally again; seeing the green fuel light blink on felt like he'd been given his life back, at least for a little while. But the fuel theft had forced him off course and now he had to relocate the Jumbo-Jumbo and its mechanical flock—and do so quickly.

But what could have been yet another crisis turned out not to be so. Praying the big mothership and its drones wouldn't divert from its last course, it took him just a few minutes of using his extraordinary eyesight to find the strange aerial formation again. And as before, the Jumbo-Jumbo's nose was still pointed southwest, and, the small arrow of UAVs was still close behind.

Once again, Hunter positioned himself two miles up and three miles behind them. Then after popping two more green pills, he settled in again.

The tail continued.

Night had fallen and the hours began to pass once again.

The stars came back out and Hunter was able to calculate his approximate position—which was still out in the middle of nowhere, with nothing but the dark Pacific below.

He'd resumed the mic-pops again. Even though he never got any response, he felt better doing them than not. He also spent a lot of time examining his instruments and double making sure everything was running to trim.

Then he went back to his go-to memories of Sara. Of Dominique. Of Viktoria Robotov.

This managed to kill several hours and did not lead him down the path that had prevented him from sleep in the recent past.

So it was a win-win . . .

Five more hours and five more pills slipped by.

The stars flew across the sky, and finally the first faint glow of the sunrise glinted off the XL's tail.

And then suddenly . . . *bloop!*

It echoed in his headphones, knocking him out of his buzzy daydreams. It was the microburst again. He looked to see the mechanical flock was finally beginning to descend.

As it did so, he began climbing—all the way up to 90,000 feet.

This was nearly twice the ceiling of a typical F-16. But the XL wasn't typical. When it was recently refurbished, a new pressurization system gave it the ability to seal up every open space anywhere on the outside of the airplane, making everything absolutely airtight. This helped the plane to fly way up in the stratified air once owned only by aircraft like the SR-71 Blackbird.

He was pretty sure no one would see him way up here.

Another addition to the restored XL's flight panel was called the VLR-FLIR/TFR. Translated: Very long-range forward-looking infra-red and terrain-following radar. It was a remarkable surveillance tool. When married to his main display's readout screen, it presented a reasonable 3-D TV image of what was happening 17 miles below.

And as soon as the screen focused, Hunter found himself looking down on a fog-enshrouded island literally in the middle of nowhere.

It was at least ten miles long and half that wide. But when he adjusted his zoom function further, he was stunned to see the island was actually an enormous air base. Five mammoth runways, dozens of smaller ones, small cities of hangars and huge supply areas. There were also fuel depots, docking facilities, vehicles and people moving everywhere—even in the dark morning hours—all under the gaze of a huge mountain on the island's western end.

Hunter's breath caught in his throat. He couldn't believe it. This was largest airbase he'd ever seen. Expertly laid out, with no wasted space, the island itself looked oddly symmetrical, as if it too had been manufactured, mountain included. Cape Kennedy might have come the closest just in sheer size. But this place was freaking enormous.

"Who the eff built this?" he said aloud.

In the postwar world any grand structures had to be bankrolled by someone or something extremely powerful. Same with the technology involved in the drones and the frighteningly enormous Jumbo-Jumbo.

The obvious conclusion: this *really* was no rag-tag operation they'd stumbled upon.

The mothership and flock did a wide turn around the island and then went into their landing profiles.

The colossal 747 touched down first, hitting one of the triple-wide runways with a cloud of dust. Legions of parachutes immediately popped out of its twin tails and winglets, helping slow the gigantic flying machine.

The drones came in right after it, buffeted by the massive plane's tailwind. They all rolled to a stop after a few dozen feet or so. Stationed in bunkers on either side of the runway, small armies of ground personnel suddenly appeared and ran to attend the unmanned aerial vehicles.

The enormous Jumbo-Jumbo never stopped moving though. Slowed down enough to taxi, it continued on a wide curving path, disappearing into an enormous cave opening in the side of the mountain.

Hunter booted up the IF level on his scope and began getting temperature readings from the island below. No surprise, the vast base was seething with heat. But he was seeing especially large temperature spikes around the mountain itself, suggesting that along with serving as a hangar for the Jumbo-Jumbo, other more extensive activities were also happening inside.

To make matters worse, his IR was showing another type of heat spike popping up all over the island. Pinpoint and static, these were weapons emplacements—anti-aircraft guns or surface-to-air missile sites, dozens, maybe more than a hundred of them on the mountainside, watching the skies above.

All of this was beyond troubling. Whether by hubris or sheer stupidity, the UA contingent just assumed that the monstrous USS *USA* would be the biggest fish in this pond. What he was seeing below put a quick end to that.

It *was* their fault. Stupidity by omission. Ever since the Russians started World War III more than a decade before, the United Americans' attention had always been turned eastward, towards the uncivilized bear. But the liberation of New York City, the destruction of the Russian secret weapons factory and then events during a second attack on Russian-occupied Hamburg put an end to all that.

So with the threat from the East diminished and with the AMC bugging out of America, a Pacific patrol in their super-cool super-carrier seemed like the right thing to do—especially when Bull offered to pick up the tab.

They didn't have a lot of intelligence on where they were going—but again that was nothing new. Every major operation they'd undertaken in the postwar world had to some degree sent them into the unknown. That's how they'd got so good at thinking and planning and fighting on the fly.

But looking down on the ginormous drone base now, Hunter popped a pill and voiced one sobering thought aloud: "How the hell do we handle this?"

Chapter Thirteen

Hunter flew over the island four more times.

Turning 360s at 90,000 feet was easy. The air was thin up here, making the banks compact and tight. As a result, he never lost the video image of the monstrous base below.

It was obvious by the third pass that the island was manmade. It might have started from a reef or a smaller atoll, but even from this height everything looked synthetic and prefab. The buildings, the hangars, the white beaches, the large perfectly round lagoon. Everything laid out with a straight edge or a French Curve.

Disney Island . . . he thought.

If the Mouse had built an air base, this is what it would look like.

But there was one thing he hadn't detected on the island: power. Or more precisely, power generating equipment. Whoever operated the vast facility would need lots of electricity because they had a lot of stuff to run down there. Despite all the heat spikes coming from within the mountain, he'd seen no smoke stacks or transmission lines anywhere. Even if they were operating off some kind of geo-thermal power or a small nuclear reactor, there would be exhaust stacks and steam vents—and both would show up big time on the FLIR.

So whatever was keeping the lights lit on the island and inside the mountain must be somewhere else.

He stayed at 90-Angels, broke out of the 360 and flew west.

He was looking for an underwater cable; it was the only way he could think of how the island could be powered. The Pacific had lots of deep spots and laying such a cable would be extremely difficult. But after seeing the facility on Disney Island, he believed its creators were capable of just about anything.

He zoomed the VLR-FLIR/TFR all the way down—and finally he saw it. Because it was warmer than its surroundings, the infra-red scope was just able to pick up its heat leak. Twisting, turning, sometimes passing out of sight completely, just to pop up again close by, at first, it looked like a snake wriggling its way through the blue Pacific. But up close he saw it was not shaped like a pipe as he'd expected. Instead it was a bright-yellow ribbon, maybe ten feet wide, a couple feet thick. He could clearly see it running along the shallow parts of the ocean floor and with such a bright shade of banana yellow, once spotted, it was really hard to miss.

So, follow the yellow brick road?

That was no problem.

It's what lay at the other end that might be tricky.

He followed the power ribbon for two hundred miles as it rippled its way west.

It was amazing how brightly yellow it was, with zero concerns about being detected. He could almost see it without the infrared gear.

Finally, out on the horizon, a string of five islands slowly came into view. They did not look manufactured in any way. The water around them got shallower as he approached, with multi-colored beds of coral and dozens of sea reefs popping up everywhere on his IR screen.

At about twenty-five miles out, the ribbon took a long turn south, leading to the first island in the chain. It was notable for its immense volcanic peak.

But where the hell was he?

The world's GPS system hadn't worked since the war. Navigating by the stars was an old art turned new. During his long night tailing of the drone swarm, he'd taken some star fixes, which only told him what he already knew. He was somewhere in the mid-Pacific.

Now with the appearance of some real land masses, the morning sun and after doing some more math, he believed he was looking down on the Solomon Islands.

*****

Closing to within ten miles, but staying up at 90-Angels, he recalibrated his VLR-FLIR/TFR and got his first close-up look of the volcanic island.

That's when his heart really sank.

Below him was an installation that put Disney Island to shame. There were five times as many buildings, roadways, vehicles, AA weapons, people and many long, white building units—all of it, an entire little city, built *inside* the huge ancient volcano.

But there was more. Zooming in on the cavernous crater he got a real shock—and also the answer to Club's meteorological question: what was causing so much heat in the troposphere along part of the Pacific Rim?

It was this place.

Inside the crater, at its middle, was a ring of twelve gigantic two-sided mirrors. They seemed as tall as skyscrapers and looked like huge, silver clipper ship sails on the VLR-FLIR/TFR. In the middle of this ring, in the middle of everything, was an even larger mirror with four separate sides.

Timing was everything, because at the moment he was looking down on it, he saw the huge four-sided mirror begin rising very slowly past the rim of the crater.

The twelve surrounding mirrors started moving as well, though painfully slow, following the rays of the morning sun as it climbed in the sky.

These were not solar panels. This was a sun farm, gigantic mirrors specially built to concentrate and then redirect the sun's rays somewhere else.

He began circling the volcanic island, his super-instincts telling him something was about to happen. Though the pace at which all thirteen of the huge, moving mirrors were turning was agonizingly and not synchronized, it all suddenly came together for him. The twelve surrounding mirrors began directing light onto the four-sided mirror tower in the middle. This in turn took those reflections, somehow concentrated them into one, enormous lightning bolt of power and shot it across the water to yet another even larger goliath-sized mirror atop another mountain on the next island over five miles to the north.

As soon as this process began, Hunter could feel the resulting heat on his own instruments—and he was 17 miles high. He had to flip down his double-sun visor it was so bright. From this height, it looked like one, long continuous streak of lightning.

He broke out of his orbit and was over the third island just seconds later. Here, he saw another spectacular sight.

This island was the biggest by far and besides being ringed by more AA sites, it housed a monstrous electrical distribution station. It literally looked like an immense car battery, easily forty stories high. On its roof was that other giant mirror. It was positioned to catch the lightning bolts coming from Mirror Island, five miles across the water.

There was no mystery in what was going on here. Whoever was running this place, they were creating immense amounts of electricity directly from the sun, then sending this power via the ribbon cable to the drone airfield on Disney Islands and who knew where else.

While solar energy technology was available before the war broke out, Hunter had never seen anything like this. It was like something from a James Bond movie.

But who was responsible for it all?

Certainly they were no friends of the AMC.

But did that mean they were allies of the UA?

He got the beginnings of his answer when he flew over the fourth island.

It was the smallest of the local chain and set back a couple miles from the others.

Unlike the three previous islands, all of which were positively crackling with energy and heat, this place was cold and damp. It was mostly denuded forest, there were no mountains or lagoons, and the surrounding beaches looked dirty and littered.

At its center was a large pit, about 1,000 feet across. The remains of another very ancient volcano, its crater lip had been beaten down over the years and was now only about a few hundred feet above the rest of the surroundings. Whatever was inside this pit was showing almost no heat at all.

As with the other islands, Hunter could see lots of boat traffic going back and forth, but the lack of any kind of facility at all on this island raised a flag with him.

"Like a graveyard," he said out loud.

The moment the words came out, he felt an unpleasant stirring in his chest, another way the cosmos sometimes sent him a message. Mirror Island was a postwar technical marvel, yet the mirrors themselves were turning in a very unsynchronized fashion? That was strange. Plus, it must have taken thousands of people to build these places and now to operate them—and to him that should smell of prosperity. Yet he wasn't looking down on any kind of tropical paradise, especially when it came to those plain white buildings inside the crater on Mirror Island.

They looked more like camps.

Concentration camps . . .

Why were the turning mirrors moving out of sync with each other, as if no mechanical device was being used?

Maybe because machines didn't turn the mirrors?

Maybe people did.

Slave labor?

Or just plain slaves?

His body really started shaking again—but it had more to do with his growing anger and apprehension.

Human slavery on a mass scale?

Is that what the cosmos was trying to tell him?

There were certainly oppressed people around the world these days. The sex-slave market had been notorious in America the first few years after the war. The Russians forced civilians to work for them during Moscow's occupation of New York City and he'd encountered other instances of slavery in his postwar travels.

But nothing like he suspected might be happening below.

If his suspicions were true, then the game would indeed change.

But he had to find out for sure.

And there was really only one way he could do it.

Fighter pilots called them drive-bys.

Get very low, turn on the external video camera, buzz the target at extremely high speed and depart with an ear-splitting sonic boom. You then clear the area and watch the footage you captured at one-quarter speed or slower.

He started slowly descending from 90-Angels. He needed time to really think about this. What he was about to do was extremely risky. He might not look like anything more than a flash of flame and exhaust going by at high speed. But whoever was running these places had a lot of AA sites which meant they must also have an air defense warning system, probably a very sophisticated one—and he was about to set off all the bells and whistles.

In rebuilding the XL, the UA flight engineers replaced a number of parts on its exterior fuselage with radar-deflecting faceted components, further cutting down on the XL's already-tiny signature, sort of bargain-basement stealth. Plus, lots of anti-aircraft weapons tended not to look straight up, because that was an unlikely direction for an attack.

But still, so far he'd done everything he could to stay hidden from the people running things on these islands.

Now, they were going to know that he was here.

He'd done more than a few of these drive-bys. They were always thrilling—but never in a good way.

Passing down through 50,000 feet, he turned on his main video camera, flipped his all-weapons switches to charge, and got the air brakes ready to go.

One last instrument check, a deep breath, two taps on his breast pocket—then he pushed the nose over, hit the afterburner and started heading straight down.

It was a very calm, typical South-Pacific morning.

Palm trees rustling in the gentle breeze, small waves lapping up on the beaches, these were the only two sounds in some places on the Solomons.

Then suddenly, a banshee scream. The shadow of an airplane falling out of the sky, spinning madly, pulling up at the very last moment, doing a lightning quick track over all the islands, and then . . . gone.

Over the horizon in the blink of an eye.

Here, but not here.

Like a flying ghost—in a part of the world where flying ghosts were thought to be gods.

Chapter Fourteen

He returned to 17 miles high, spiraling straight up on full burner.

Leveling out, he pulled back to 300 knots, went into another mile-tight 360 then engaged the autopilot. With all systems showing green, he called up his external cam's video footage. No need for infrared enhancement here. He wanted to see it raw.

He dialed the tape speed down to ten percent and started the video rolling. He'd gone over the Mirror Island first, not 100 feet above the crater at 1,800 miles per hour. The low-tape speed was essential here, he'd been moving so fast.

But almost immediately it was like watching the most horrible kind of horror movie—in super-slow motion. In the next few seconds, he saw things he could never unsee, not to his dying day.

Slaves were indeed turning the skyscraper high mirrors. But these things were more than gigantic up close, so a *lot* of slave power was needed to move just one of them—and keep it moving. To do this, hundreds of dark-skinned people, dressed in rags and strapped together, were pulling on long lines of thick rope. Each towering mirror had a giant spool and sprocket assembly in front of it, both made of wood, which had to be attached to some really big gears somewhere. By continuously pulling on the ropes, the spool moved the sprocket, which in turn moved the monstrous mirror.

Hunter froze the tape and counted as best he could how many people it took to do this, having the giant mirror follow the sun across the sky in a place that rarely saw a cloudy day. He stopped at three hundred, just on one rope. Times twelve mirrors, there had to be at least 3,600 slaves down there, working in the relentless heat.

Making it all worse, he could see dozens of guards overseeing the brutal operation. Some were walking the perimeter of the crater, others were in guard towers. But many were right down with the slaves—whipping them.

Hunter didn't need to look at it for more than a few seconds. He fast forwarded the tape to his next photo target: Battery Island, with its giant mirror and huge storage station.

But, again, he took only a few seconds to study it; there were very few people on this island, unless its operations were underground. Either way, he knew what its function was. He fast forwarded again.

It was the next island that ran a chill through him.

The island with no life on it. No heat. Nothing . . .

One glimpse confirmed his worst fears. This place was an island of the dead . . . literally. The huge pit was filled with bodies. Hundreds of them—and he was sure they were mostly worn-out slaves. After how many hours of merciless toil, this was where they ended up. In a pit, probably to be doused with fuel and lit up every so often, turning the dead weight into ashes and bones.

He froze the tape again, sickened by what he was seeing.

Yet, in the strangest way, he felt vindicated, for himself and the UA.

This was pure evil.

And at that moment, all the ambiguity and the what-are-we-doing-out-here stuff went up in smoke.

Now he *knew* why they were out here.

This, they had to do something about.

His body never really stopped trembling. Not from the result of a shot of clairvoyance, but with pure anger.

And that was okay, because the adrenalin helped him plan out, in sequence, what he had to do next.

Turn east, fly about an hour at close to burner speed and get back in radio contact with the *USA*. Request a trio of buddy tankers get airborne, rendezvous with them, do a daisy chain back to the carrier—and *then* decide how to handle this.

But then, unexpectedly, a strange noise filled his ears. A pulsating tone, urgent and irritating at the same time.

It took a moment to realize what it was: his defensive suite was telling him an antiaircraft missile had locked onto the XL. *This* was why the noise was so foreign to him. He wasn't sure he'd ever heard it before.

But that feeling only lasted a moment.

He pulled the stick right and just tumbled away. Wing over wing, nose over end, he went down through 85,000 feet, 80,000 . . .

He pulled back at 75-Angels, stopped the spinning and hit the throttle.

But the tone was still in his ears . . .

And something else was happening now too. Looking behind him, he caught the quickest glimpse of a jet fighter just coming out of a free fall, perfectly mimicking Hunter's maneuver after the Wingman had dodged its first missile.

In the next second, this plane launched two more missiles at him. Hunter pulled hard right once again, disrupting the air flow in front of the lead missile, causing it to spin away off course.

But the second missile blew up very close to him.

Again, he was able to take pre-emptive action and hit his throttle just in time so as not to take a lot of damage. But this was not good.

Someone was still locked on his six o'clock, the most vulnerable position for a fighter pilot. The warning klaxon was suddenly in his ears again. It was such a foreign sound! But it was telling him more missiles were on the way.

He dropped his nose again and this time went straight down. The shock was wearing off. It was such a new experience to be on the wrong side of a dogfight, it had taken him a few moments to get his act together.

Fully recovered, in the next second he did five things almost at once. Flip the all-weapons switch back to charge. Punch the aux-power button to on. Turn on the head up display. Tighten his harness to max. Pop a green pill.

At last, he was ready to fight.

Now . . . who was screwing with him up here?

He pushed the stick sideways and did a very tight turn. Suddenly he was looking right at his opponent. He was about a quarter mile to his starboard and turning into him.

Pow! Another punch to the gut. But this one only lasted a moment, because suddenly it all made total sense.

This one . . . his internal radar never picked up. He never saw it coming.

It was the Ghost Plane of LA. The mysterious black fighter that had caused so much chaos over the AMC evacuation ships that night.

Now here it was again. Trying to bust caps with him . . .

Cook and the JAWS guys had been right. It was a Russian-built Su-27 Flanker fighter, its look and lineage very similar to the Su-34 attack planes the UA flew off the carrier. But this bird had never carried a bomb in its life. It was a pure gunslinger, all missiles and cannons, shiny black from nose to nozzles.

They zoomed by each other, and in that moment, Hunter was able to size up his attacker. He didn't care who he was or who he was flying for. Getting shot at was a very personal experience and an infuriating one. Even more so if the shot missed. An old Irish saying went: "Revenge is the best revenge." And Hunter was part Irish.

So, this clown was going down.

He armed all his missiles—eight Sidewinders. He switched on his cannon lamp; the six M61 rotary guns sticking out of his nose immediately came to life, ready to fire.

Now, exactly how to do this?

They were still around 75,000 feet—really no place for a dogfight. But sometimes you couldn't pick your battlefield.

He pushed the stick hard left now, went into a quick loop and was suddenly just where he wanted to be—right on the Flanker's tail. The black jet began zig zagging, trying to avoid the XL's missile lock, but it was not working.

Hunter heard the magic tone confirming two of his Sidewinders had the Flanker in their electronic sights and were ready to go.

But in that instant—before he could squeeze the launch button—he suddenly went blind.

One moment, no problem.

The next, he couldn't see a thing.

Instinct took over. He pulled back the throttle, cutting his speed by half.

Three long seconds went by, a slight panic rising inside him until—just as suddenly, his vision returned.

He was shaking again, and the reason was hardly cosmic this time. His eyes adjusted, slowly, almost painfully, but soon he could see the controls again. And then the outside world came back into view and looked somewhat normal again.

What happened?

It was like a giant flash bulb had gone off in his face. Fighting the direct sun was a hazard every dogfighter faced. But he'd never been blinded by the sun's glare before.

He'd lost the missile lock on the Flanker, but was still behind him. He made up for those few seconds by kicking in the burner, putting him back on his opponent's tail.

For the second time, he selected two of his Sidewinders and heard the missile lock tone in return.

But once again, he was a microsecond away from firing when there was another blindingly bright flash of light. He was ready this time. His body had started buzzing just an instant before the second beam would have gone directly into his eyes. Hunter thanked the cosmos for his enhanced intuition once more—because without it, he surely would have been blinded again, maybe permanently.

Still it was like a near collision with a bolt of lightning. The flash was so powerful all of the XL's panel lights started blinking. He pulled hard left, further distancing himself from the deadly beam. Then he began spinning on purpose, trying to shake off the bad electromagnetics caused by the near miss with the death ray. About half his instruments popped back on by the time he passed through 65,000 feet.

Finally, he leveled off and took five deep gulps of oxygen.

One time was very strange—twice in the span of just a few seconds and it suddenly wasn't so strange anymore.

The Flanker wasn't fighting fair. In addition to all the weapons stores he had aboard, the black jet's pilot was also somehow able to manipulate one of the gigantic mirrors below and use its concentrated light against him.

Viktor Robotov, Hunter's arch enemy, recently departed, once developed a nuclear warhead that, when detonated, would blind anybody unlucky enough to be looking at it, so bright was its blast. The people running the gigantic mirror operation simply took Einstein out of that equation. They were able to use the sunlight to gather power. But they were also able to use it as a weapon.

Hunter fell away to 55,000 feet; this was where the Flanker wound up after the second lightning attack. On his way down, the Wingman started doing some calculations. The Flanker pilot or someone he was working with on the ground was able to send the lightning bolts his way—and it had been a close call both times.

But they weren't actually shooting these things at him; rather they were redirecting the sun's concentrated energy and sending it into his path.

This meant he had to keep his back to the sun, believing simple physics said it would be harder for them to direct anything at him from that direction.

But unlike in the movies, where dogfights were usually shown as being horizontal, in reality most were fought in three dimensions, especially in the true vertical, going straight up or straight down.

Hunter saw the Flanker pan out at 52,000 feet and start a tight turn; in seconds he was coming right at him, an explosion of flame from his tail pipe being the telltale sign that the Flanker pilot had kicked in his afterburner.

But Hunter knew this game.

It was the opening move of the famous Cobra maneuver. Pull up at the last moment, go into the hovering act, allow your opponent to rocket by you, and then loop over, go back down and get on his ass.

There really was only one way to counter it. Hunter turned and pointed his nose at the Flanker. An instant later, when the black jet went into its circus trick, Hunter did too.

But catching on quick, the Flanker booted throttles and just kept climbing—and so did Hunter. Suddenly, both of them were going straight up, on afterburner, each matching the other's speed exactly.

This started around 52-Angels, but they passed through 80,000 just seconds later. Again, in the thinness of the rarified air, you could go faster and burn less fuel, for a while. But, going nose up in any aircraft meant you were battling gravity at its most powerful, and because less air meant less lift, no matter what you did, at some point gravity wins the battle and it's only a matter of time before your engine stalls out.

No pilot wants that ever, never mind in the middle of a dogfight. So it becomes a game of chicken. Whoever flinches, whoever gives up and heads back down first, is just going to be pursued and most likely shot down by the guy who had the bigger stones.

But another sign that this might not be a typical furball was when both pilots turned outwards by 45-degrees at the exact same moment.

Suddenly they were wing to wing and could see each other up close. His opponent was dressed all in black of course, looking out at him like some dark knight of the skies. Hunter just stared back at him.

Eyes still locked, they went past 90-Angels in a blur.

95,000 . . .

The magical 100K . . .

110 . . .

120 . . .

No airplane was made for this and it would be a testament to the almost paranormal aspect of this contest that both participants' engines stalled at exactly the same time.

Within seconds, *both* were falling back towards earth, out of control.

The one good thing about stalling out at twenty-three miles up is you had a long way down to figure out how not to crash. Restarting his engine was Hunter's prime mission, but he also knew he had to do it without the Flanker winding up on his tail.

This called for something very creative.

Passing back down through 95-Angels, he went hard right everything, and managed to stop his spin. In that same instant he took a deep gulp of oxygen and pushed the nose straight over. Like riding down a miles-long roller-coaster hill, he held it steady as the ocean rushed up at him with tremendous speed.

Ten seconds . . . fifteen, easily five gs.

Twenty seconds, six gs, going more than 1400 knots now, absolutely straight down.

Then, two more gulps of O, and at 40,000 feet he deployed his RAT, another gizmo his New York friends had installed on the XL. RAT stood for Ram-Air Turbine. It was a small device looking not unlike a desk fan which deployed out of the nose. It was actually a mini-wind turbine, because as soon as it began spinning, it started producing electricity.

He passed down through 25,000 feet, then twenty, then fifteen . . .

He watched as the power boost began to grow, starting a few things on his control board. Finally, it reached 220 volts, in theory enough electricity to restart his engine.

Another deep breath, then on the count of three, he pushed his power start button and hit the afterburner. There was a loud bang—and the smell of fumes filled his cockpit. But suddenly, his engine was running again.

Suddenly, he was back in control—sort of.

In a dogfight, they say the plane that's been shot down and plunging to earth, "meets its shadow" when it crashes. Hunter could actually see the shadow of the XL on the Pacific Ocean, coming at him at very high speed.

Finally, he pulled back on the stick with all his might and took the eight gs like a man.

Hold your breath, marry that stick . . .

An instant later, he was flying level again, doing 600 knots, not fifty feet above the waves. And right up ahead of him, coming in the opposite direction, was the Black Flanker.

Hunter pulled back on the stick and hit the throttles. And so did the Flanker's pilot.

And just like that, they were climbing again, only to stall again, fall again, and start all over.

It went on like this for more than five minutes. Up and down. Back and forth. Barrel Rolls. Hi Yo-Yos. Flat Scissors. Immelmann Turns. They performed every fighter pilot trick in the book on each other, but nothing worked. In that time, Hunter became certain of just one thing: Whoever this guy was, he was by far the best dogfighter he'd ever gone up against.

Every move he made, his opponent came up with the perfect countermove.

The fight entered Round Two when both planes, their pilots exhausted, met each other at 55,000 feet.

Five more minutes of intense air combat followed. Hunter unleashed all of his Sidewinders in that time—but to no effect. He had missile lock tones with every barrage, but the Flanker did what Hunter himself would have done in the same case. He waited until the very last moment before the missile arrived and then just turned over and fell out of the sky. Depending on your altitude, if you lived through the dead dog maneuver, you would confuse a missile's warhead every time.

In the same five minutes, the Flanker had unleashed a total of four more air-to-air missiles at the XL—and Hunter countered them the exact same way.

Only after each plane had expended its missiles did round three begin.

Now all they had were their cannons. This meant close in combat, brutal and usually bloody. It's when a dogfight turns really nasty.

Like two knights in armor in an aerial jousting match, they did endless cannon runs on each other—with neither one scoring any hits. Hunter had more guns—six cannons in his nose, compared the Flanker's two. But the Russian-built plane carried more ammunition and had a higher rate of fire. Knowing this, Hunter tried to make every burst count, but again it was like he was fighting a mirror image of himself.

They were down in the grass at this point, banging away at each other at barely 5,000 feet. To avoid one fusillade from the Flanker, Hunter engaged in a very risky, Split-S maneuver at this very low altitude.

It usually takes about 4,000-foot clearance for a jet to perform a split-S. Hunter did it in less than 1,000, creating bizarre vapor trails as he did so. And finally, by doing this, he once again wound up on the Flanker's tail.

This was it, what the longest ten minutes in his life had been all about, knocking this guy out of the air.

All he had to do was squeeze the trigger . . .

That's when he got hit with another lightning bolt.

It was just like the first two, except this one blinded him completely for ten terrifying seconds. In that time, taking advantage of the poor sportsmanship, the Black Flanker came at him broadside and filled the nose of the newly refurbished XL full of holes. The cannon shells hit with such force, it spun the superjet sideways and then completely over. Suddenly Hunter was going down, straight down, upside down with no engine, no power, no weapons—and no sight. Plus, half his canopy was missing. Shattered by the Flanker's cannon barrage, the wind was blowing in his face at hurricane speed.

By manipulating his rudders, though, he managed to turn himself right side up—and at that same moment his vision cleared once again. But the XL's main flight controls were shot up to the point he wasn't really flying anymore, more like gliding. His heart was breaking, too—all that work the New York guys did in rebuilding the XL and now he'd fucked it up again.

He went down through 4,000 feet, losing altitude fast. Before finishing him off, the Flanker came down close beside him, not 20 feet off his wing. This allowed the pilot to give Hunter one last, mocking salute before shooting him down for good.

But that's when the Flanker pilot saw something completely unexpected. The American pilot was aiming something at him through the cracked glass of his canopy.

It was a massive handgun. A .357 Magnum, to be precise.

He tried to pull back on the throttle, but it was too late. The American fired five times, hitting five of the most vital systems in the Flanker pilot's control suite. A moment later, his entire flight panel blew up right in front of him.

Suddenly, the Flanker was going down too.

Chapter Fifteen

Another option installed in the XL by the New York City restoration team was called the NASA Fix.

Hunter always fought on the edge. Because they didn't want to see their refurbished masterpiece wrecked again, the New York guys installed five enormous parachutes filched from the old Cape Kennedy. Designed to bring the Apollo astronauts safely back to Earth, each was almost 100 feet across and together, could bring the XL to a relatively soft landing.

Just moments after firing his .357 Magnum at the Flanker, mortally wounding it, Hunter hit his new ELS switch. Instantly, the five big chutes deployed from a midway point on his upper fuselage. Five violent jolts followed, but the chutes did their job. One moment he was in the process of crashing—the next he was level and floating.

He had no idea where he was. The dogfight had lasted more than ten minutes, an eternity in a business where the first shot usually won. They could have easily strayed 500 miles in any direction.

But not a minute after his chutes went up, through the mists, a small atoll come into view. It was surrounded by a ring of fog, had a lagoon in the middle and two peaks on its far side.

Oddly familiar, Hunter thought.

His engine had shut down; his flight controls had been damaged by the Flanker's final attack, but he was still able to manually work his airplane's flaps.

It wasn't exact and it wasn't pretty, but it was enough to steer himself safely towards the misty island.

He landed on the western side of the lagoon, floating in through the ring of fog and coming down with a hard bump atop a bed of cracked oyster shells.

The five big chutes immediately collapsed on top of the damaged XL; it was never part of any plan, but the sandy-colored silks camouflaged it perfectly.

It took him twenty minutes to unstrap and fight his way out of the overlapping billows, though. He finally crawled out under the port side wing, more exhausted than when he was in the middle of the dogfight.

No matter. He popped a green pill, took a swig from his canteen and that was that.

He took a long look around, his eyes finally focusing on the island's twin peaks. Rising up next to the eastern-side summit was a long column of gray smoke.

The Flanker's crash site.

That's where he had to go.

*****

Walking over the oyster beds was the hardest part.

He'd kept his helmet on and his boots tied tight, because stumbling on these things would be like falling down on a field of broken glass.

He made it at last, crossed the lagoon and headed into the jungle. Not six months before, he'd crash landed on another fog-enshrouded tropical island. But that was in the Bermuda Triangle. This place was different. Hot, lots of lush flora, humid, misty, these things they'd shared in common. But there was definitely a different vibe here. Everything was just a little more intense.

He scaled the mountain via a series of paths leading to the summit. Once at the top he was able to look down onto the other side of the island—and that's where he saw it.

The Flanker he'd just shot down. It was twenty yards offshore, in shallow water. Smoking heavily, its tail section on fire, it was going through its death throes. Its cockpit was crushed and, dead or alive, he could see the pilot was still inside.

It was only at that moment that Hunter finally stopped. Stopped moving, stopped thinking. Stopped everything but breathing.

It was over.

He was exhausted. He was lost. His plane was wrecked again.

But, he'd won.

And . . . it was over.

For about two seconds. Because then he saw movement inside the crushed cockpit even as the fire started to spread from the tail section towards the front. Then he heard someone scream.

"Son of a bitch," he said. "*This* bullshit again?"

The next thing he knew he was running down the side of the mountain, down three more paths, into the jungle, onto the beach—and into the water.

As sometimes happened to him in times of heightened awareness, everything went into slow motion when in fact he was moving as fast as he could.

He fought his way through the steam and smoke and found the plane in about four feet of water. The cockpit was full of smoke, but he could hear coughing and could see movement inside.

Like the Su-34, the Flanker had a duckbill nose. It carried a lot of gear in it and it was that gear that lay crumpled in the coral blue water. The lip of the canopy top had detached itself from the wrecked nose and the electronics inside would sizzle anytime a wave hit them.

Hunter had broken into his share of crashed jet cockpits. It was always a gamble. If you managed to bust one of the glass panels, you could possibly feed the flames with wind and oxygen and the whole plane could go up. Or, if you did get through the glass, and if the pilot was unconscious or stuck, you had to climb in the cockpit yourself and try to free them, all while fire was making its way toward you and knowing it would eventually hit something highly flammable and then the rodeo would be over.

Studying the situation for about a half second, Hunter put his hands under the lip of the canopy and started to lift it . . . only to have the canopy suddenly open on its own.

That's when he found himself staring down the barrel of a Russian-made T-33 pistol.

Chapter Sixteen

"How many times do I have to tell you? You're irrelevant. I'm irrelevant. We're fighter pilots. Our day is done . . ."

Hunter was sitting on the beach, just off where the Flanker had plowed in. His hands were tied behind him with electrical wire. He was trying his best to get free, but his captor had doubled and tripled tied him up, so it was going to be a long process.

Meanwhile he was being tortured. Not physically, but mentally for having to listen to his captor go on and on . . . and on . . . about himself.

He'd been an air merc since his teens. He'd fought mostly for Russia in that time, until he was hired for a fortune by the people who ran the slave camps. Protecting the big mirrors was just one part of his job. Another part involved harassing the AMC ships in LA harbor, and then tracking them after they left, so his employers could murder them all in the most appalling fashion.

But it was Hunter's misfortune that the pilot, possibly taking his own brand of little green pills, not only wouldn't shut up, but insisted on expounding on his philosophical views including the one that hit Hunter particularly hard in the gut: the fighter pilot as a dying breed.

"The world changed the moment the Big War began," the Flanker pilot said, in so many words, more than once. "Sure, as pilots, we fought. We were part of the force. But a lot of us got shot down flying our very expensive airplanes, and even with everything going to hell very quickly, a lot of people out there said, there's got to be a better way."

At this point, the pilot looked out endearingly on his smacked-down Flanker, its skeleton slowly burning away in the shallow tide.

"For the money it costs to build one of those," he said. "They can build a thousand drones. Two thousand even, maybe three. If ninety-nine percent get shot down, but one percent gets through, it's mission accomplished—with no expensive-to-train pilots lost.

"It's the numbers, my friend. You can't fool the numbers . . ."

He was dressed in all black. Flight suit, boots, gloves, visor and helmet, which he didn't take off—but it was all a bit cliché at this point. In between haranguing about the last days of the fighter pilot, he claimed the people who ran Mirror Island had also hired him to lure the great Wingman out to the South Pacific where he would be disposed of, for a sizable bonus.

In other words, he was a true mercenary—and a damn good pilot.

But after ten minutes, Hunter was ready to explode, so sick he was of listening to the *braggadocio*.

"So why do you do what you do?" he finally spit back at him.

The pilot man shrugged. He was holding the T-33 pistol on Hunter, but doing so very casually. He had barely frisked him once they both reached the shore, finding his survival knife and nothing more. It was obvious the man liked to hear the sound of his own voice, which had only the slightest Russian accent. That seemed to be his first priority.

"Why do I do what I do?" he asked, repeating the question. "To be the last gunslinger, I guess . . ."

Hunter just laughed at him. "I just shot you down, remember?"

"True, but first, I'll spin it so it was a tie," the pilot said through his full helmet visor. "Then as the years go on, I'll keep changing my story until, I guarantee you, history will state that I was the victor here."

"And I won't be around to clear things up?" Hunter asked him more out of exasperation than anything else.

The pilot just shrugged. "It will be less inconvenient that way," he replied.

He looked out at his plane again—it was almost a total wreck by now.

"Anyway, it will be easy to manipulate the narrative, as they say," he went on. "The truth only survives where it's allowed to. And those days are quickly coming to an end too. These ideas that you Americans have about democracy and personal freedom—they're as outdated as manned aircraft. People need to be ruled with a strong hand. They need to be told what to do. So, you and your friends have been fighting all this time for nothing. The new wave is that there are people on top and then there's the rest of everybody. You kneel on their necks until they get the message. So forget all those American ideals, because . . ."

At that moment Hunter got his hands free and, all in one fluid motion, pulled his .357 Magnum from his boot holster and shot the Flanker pilot once in the head.

The man coughed and then fell over, dead before he hit the ground.

Chapter Seventeen

He dug the grave with his bare hands.

Six feet deep in the wet sand, his fingernails were bleeding by the end of it, cut and scraped by so many broken oyster shells.

It took him three hours, two feet an hour, and twice as many pills. He wasn't really there though. It was like he was watching someone else dig madly in the sand. Meanwhile, his mind was somewhere else . . .

The little green pills made him high—yet he'd never felt so low. He'd never killed anyone in cold blood before. Never knew how it would feel. He had his reasons. He just couldn't allow the Flanker pilot to distort what had happened here. He knew enough about himself—and how people thought of him—that if the last word anyone heard about The Wingman was that some Russian merc had finally shot him down, then the ideals that he'd worked for ever since the Big War and even earlier, might also go down in flames.

That was one side anyway.

The other side was darker. Maybe it was his ego and not so much his ideals that wanted the world to know who won this fight. And that he was still the best fighter pilot who ever lived.

His blood stream flowing with whatever chemicals the little green pills contained, he couldn't settle on which side was the truth and it was tearing him up inside.

And it only got stranger. Because before he put the Flanker pilot in his grave, he lifted the dead man's helmet visor, a cyclone of voices inside his conscience telling him at the very least he had to see the face of the man he'd killed.

But when he did, when he lifted the shield and saw the features of the dead man, it was like staring at himself through a bloody mirror.

They looked exactly the same.

The dead man could have been his twin.

It was past sunset before he was done.

Exhausted, strung out, lost and terribly alone, he started to climb the mountain again, intent on getting to the peak, and as far away from the beach as possible.

It took almost an hour to scale the heights; he was so disconnected he could barely put one foot in front of the other. And no matter where he looked, he could only see darkness.

Until he got to the top of the mountain, that is—and found someone was waiting for him.

She was wearing a plaid shirt, jeans and a white baseball cap. She was standing there, almost a little impatiently, but smiling at him nonetheless.

It was her. Literally the girl from his dreams, the memory he'd tried so hard to forget—and failed—was now right here, standing in front of him.

For a moment, he wondered if maybe he'd actually lost the dogfight and that it was he who was dead. But in the same instant, he knew he was wrong because his heart felt like it was beating right out of his chest.

She was an angel, but he was still very much alive.

They didn't speak. He just crumpled at her feet, and she came down beside him and held him for the entire night.

She was gone when he woke up.

It took a while for that to sink in, but once he'd accepted it, the first thing he did was throw the rest of his pills off the cliff and into the ocean, never to take anything like them again.

He watched them disappear into the morning ring of fog. But suddenly, by the most fortunate breeze, a hole opened up in the thick mist and he could see the eastern horizon.

And, way, way out, just coming into his sightline, was the massive outline of the USS *USA*.

In the next moment, he heard an oddly familiar sound. It was the brutish noise coming from a Beriev Be-4 Russian-built seaplane, an aircraft he'd flown during his adventure on that lost and foggy Bermuda island. Wildly wagging its wings, it flew right over him, so close he could see Ben Wa was behind the controls.

Then another noise—that of a helicopter. A Russian-built but thoroughly Americanized Hind gunship, with the roundel and stripes emblem of the United Americans crudely painted on it, also came out of the mist. It too was soon right over him.

He looked up to see Crunch and JT were flying the thing and Crunch was yelling down to him.

"Hey, Hawk! You need a ride?"

PART THREE

Return of the Gods

Chapter Eighteen

It was called an IFF.

Identification, Friend or Foe. It was a device that sent out a radio beacon containing information on whether an aircraft was military or civilian, friendly or not. Basically, two radios talking to each other, IFF could also determine range and bearing, and therefore the distance, between two aircraft.

So, although the USS *USA* had stopped getting Hunter's mic-pops hours before, because they were sailing towards his last known location, the air crews were told to begin searching for the XL's IFF signal. It took some triangulation and no small amount of luck—plus cranking up the engines inside the mammoth carrier and pushing them to an astounding 55 knots. But when morning cleared, one of the CAP planes picked up the signal and led the carrier right to the tiny island.

He was helicoptered aboard, along with his damaged XL, to the great relief of everyone. Deferring any medical attention or food, he gave the recon tape to Dozer and then disappeared into the bowels of the huge carrier along with an unlikely pair of colleagues.

The wide-ranging automation on board the *USA* allowed most of the crew to crowd into the naval war room and watch the recon video the Wingman had shot during his high-speed drive-by of the small string of Solomon Islands.

But anyone in the room with a predilection towards vertigo was in for an unpleasant surprise. The tape began just as Hunter was turning the XL over at 50,000 feet and what followed was footage of the super-jet rocketing straight down on full afterburner, spinning wing over wing for good measure. Like something viewed from a very high amusement ride, the earth kept getting bigger with each spiraling moment. Then, at what looked to be the last possible instant, the XL pulled up from the impossibly-fast dive in just a matter of microseconds.

In all, the controlled plummet took just six seconds, and it was head-spinning for anyone watching.

Then just 100 feet off the deck—at three times the speed of sound—he started his high-speed pass over the necklace of islands.

In real time, Hunter had rocketed over the entire chain in just seven seconds. But Tony 3's high-speed/high resolution VCR was able to provide a playback as slow as one frame per second in color and with impressive clarity.

What they saw would change their lives.

Mirror Island and its gargantuan mobile reflectors, the huge storage device on Battery Island, the impossibly gruesome happenings on Death Pit Island.

The concentrated light going between the two islands, caught at the edge of a few video frames, was so intense it had a kind of rainbow surrounding it. An aura, almost.

The ship's weatherman, Commander Keefe, was in attendance and finally, he had his answer to what was causing the high temperatures and an occasional man-made Aurora Borealis above parts of the Pacific Rim.

It's just that he couldn't believe it.

None of them could. Ian Fleming couldn't have dreamed it up any better . . .

But something very real was going on here.

They could clearly see the evidence of both slavery and genocide. Just the one slo-mo pass over the Death Pit Island was enough to record people being tossed into the open quarry, some fighting desperately as they were still alive.

Some of them women and small children.

Hunter was four decks below the war room, in one of the engineering shops. Tony 3 was there. So was Lieutenant Ruggeri, the CO of Slugboat 7.

The armed tug had played a main role in two things that had happened the morning the AMC fleet was attacked. First, it had collided with one of the drones and had dragged it aboard, just seconds before the main force of UAVs struck. But thirty minutes later, just as it was arriving back at the carrier, it was asked to disentangle the dead AMC soldier from the ship's anchor chain and leeward line. They were able to pull the body free of the anchor, but it was hopelessly caught up in the line and wound up being hauled aboard.

The body was now down in the ship's cold storage, just recently examined by the carrier's medical team. The drone itself, though, was on a table in front of them. They were conducting an autopsy on it.

Once pulled apart, Tony examined every piece, anxious to see what made it tick. He took ten minutes in complete silence just studying the nose cone of the UAV. There was a massive jumble of wires inside the crushed muzzle, most of them connected to a pocket calculator.

It looked impossibly complex to make any sense, but somehow Tony was able to figure it out.

"Basically, if all their drones are like this, then they're controlled via the Radio Data System or RDS," he said finally. "You mentioned you heard a blooping noise, Hawk? That's RDS at work, sending out a radio burst. It's a simple system. They're all just flying radio receivers with built-in memories—that's why the pocket calculator.

The first guys to land on the moon used a computer with less memory than that little baby right there.

"They receive the radio burst, it sounds like a bloop, but it's really just a bunch of elementary commands that the drone will obey, each one in order, when the time is right. For most of them, that last radio command is 'dive' and that starts their whole kamikaze routine. But other commands are needed for takeoff, aerial refueling and landing—if you make it back that is."

"But those hunter-killer bugs," Hunter said. "The ones with the machine guns on board, they seemed pretty sophisticated, shooting all those mooks in the water."

"I know it seems that way," Tony explained. "But their particular commands are just saying: go back and forth at low level inside a certain area, fire your guns at prearranged times and if enough of you do this, eventually you'll kill everything on the surface, or anything the sharks didn't get to first. I'm going to guess that maybe a dozen or so of those drones had cheap video cameras installed so whoever was doing all this could see what was happening in real time."

"From a plane somewhere overhead?" Hunter asked.

"Wouldn't have to be," Tony said. "If it's using shortwave, it could have been two or three hundred miles away at the time.

"But it's nothing more than the miracle of radio. That's how they make these things fly, that's how they make them do what they do. The basic concept would work on any airplane. Tune into the right frequency, feed it an assemblage of the right commands, have someone somewhere doing the fine tuning. It's not rocket science, because it doesn't have to be."

"Is there any limit to the number of drones you can control like this?" Ruggeri asked.

Tony just shook his head no. "If they're all on the same frequency and behaving as they've been programmed, there's no limit. Plus, they're so cheap you can send a bunch on a mission, and even if the majority screws up, you still have a lot of these bad boys coming your way."

"None of this is pleasant to hear," Hunter said dryly. "But at least now we know exactly what message they were sending us by creaming the AMC right in front of our noses."

"Yeah, this could be you," Ruggeri said. "Can you imagine having hundreds of these things falling out of the sky over LA or San Francisco just like they did on the AMC fleet?"

Tony laughed darkly.

"'Hundreds?'" he asked. "You can build these things for about three bucks each. And judging by the kind of sophistication of those island installations you saw, Hawk—we've got to think these guys could put up thousands of these things. Maybe even *tens* of thousands.

"And if that's true, they could pull off something on our West Coast that would make Pearl Harbor look like a picnic . . ."

Chapter Nineteen

Thirty minutes later, Hunter and Dozer were walking near the very tip of the carrier's ski-jump flight deck.

They, along with the rest of the crew, had just finished a FOD drill—for Foreign Object Damage drill. As frequently as possible, the entire deck of the USS *USA* had to be scanned for any loose debris that might pose a hazard to the jet intakes of departing or incoming aircraft. If sucked into a jet engine, even the smallest screw could cause a catastrophe, blowing up the plane, igniting its fuel and cooking off its weapons.

The FOD drill was completed just as the sun was going down. Hunter flipped a few loose bolts he'd found over the side, then he and his old friend sat on the edge of the lower foredeck walkway, looking out at the vast Pacific. Dusk had arrived.

Hunter took a moment to brief him on the drone autopsy, or at least the preliminaries anyway. The UAVs were cheap, controllable from a long distance and apparently plentiful. Just like what happened during the twin attacks on the AMC fleet, fighting them successfully would be close to impossible. It was all in the numbers.

They both knew most military missions were fraught with unexpected twists—and that few of them were ever pleasant. But this one had twisted itself right into the twilight zone. They'd apparently stumbled upon a vast South Pacific empire which could not only harness immense amounts of the sun's energy to make power, but also to use as a weapon. And they still had no idea who these people were.

Yet, the evidence of slavery and genocide was so clear, it didn't really matter. The UA just couldn't stand by and let them do all this unhindered for the same old reason: To do so would be un-American. Besides, they were now in the thick of it—especially if whoever was running the drones discovered that the USS *USA* hadn't got their message and was still in the area.

They were both quiet for another few minutes, looking out on the dark Pacific waves with uncertainty in every breath. A bright flash lit up the horizon off to the west. It was the manmade Aurora, exciting atoms all over in the night sky, a painful reminder of what kind of opponent they were up against.

But they both shrugged when they saw it. They were tired, overworked and a long, long way from home. They really didn't need the cosmos to tell them what was waiting for them out there.

Finally, Dozer just asked him: "What happened back on that island, Hawk? Who was that guy you said you were tangling with?"

Hunter didn't speak for nearly a minute.

Only then did he say, "That's a story for another time . . ."

Chapter Twenty

After not sleeping for almost three days, Dozer finally hit the rack and suggested Hunter should do the same.

But the Wingman headed for the War Room instead. He sat there alone, watching his drive-by recon tape over and over.

With each replay, something very deep inside told him something he did not want to know: that what he was seeing was the new normal in this part of the world. It wouldn't be the first empire built on the backs of free, disposable labor—but, as bad as things were, he never thought he'd see things like this.

Maybe he'd been asleep all this time. Maybe he'd just dreamed about the raid on Viktor's secret arctic base. Maybe winning New York City back from the Russians had just been a reverie—one of those memories that seems so real at the time, only to prove to be a flight of fantasy a second or two later.

Maybe none of it was real.

Because what he saw on this slowed-down tape seemed like civilization in reverse. All the vileness they fought and finally won against in America, was alive and kicking over here, just an ocean away. Were they so blinded by the red, white and blue that they weren't aware of the big picture? If this was going on in other parts of the globe, what good was freedom in America? How long could it last?

Son of a bitch . . . he thought

His doppelganger had been right.

The world was going through an enormous change and if they didn't get right with it now, then they'd for sure wind up on the outside, looking in.

Suddenly Hunter wished he was back home with his girlfriend Sara, just hanging.

In the next moment, he wondered if he would ever get to do that again.

They were facing a gigantic task here.

If they chose to accept it, they had to be very smart about it and that usually meant trying to get as much intelligence on the target and the surrounding area as possible and use it to their advantage.

So he went over the videotape a dozen times, looking for something, anything, that might offer a ray of hope in the otherwise dark situation.

It turned out thirteen was his lucky number—because during the thirteenth viewing of the tape, he saw something he hadn't seen before.

Something that would change everything,

He'd actually flown over four islands during his supersonic drive-by. About a mile north of the Death Pit island was another atoll set way off from the others. Dark and foreboding, it was covered in jungle, hardly had any beaches surrounding it and appeared uninhabited.

Its most distinctive feature was the high plateau on its western edge. It was this part of the landscape that just happened to get captured on video tape just before Hunter clicked off the camera and started his screaming climb back to up 17 miles high. The plateau was flat and covered in green grass, almost giving the impression of a small baseball field. Half of it had been masked by the climbing morning sun's shadows, and the XL was over the tiny island for less than a second.

But the videotape picked up something interesting, something it took Hunter to see thirteen times before he realized it was looking at something out of the ordinary. Freeze-framing the video, he studied it closely.

Located in the center of the grassy field was a crudely built symbol of some kind. At first he thought it was a cross—or maybe even a crucifix. He guessed it was about thirty feet long.

But then he noticed there was a small cross section towards the end of the object.

It looked like a tail fin.

And that's when it became clear.

This wasn't a cross or a crucifix.

This was something purposely built to look like an airplane.

Thirty seconds later, he buzzed Dozer's cabin, waking him up.

"I think I have a plan . . ." he said.

Chapter Twenty-One

The next day

Chief Bateri had a story to tell.

It began during World War II more than six decades earlier. Bateri's great-grandfather was chief of the Tannus back then and the tribe worked for the American army who were fighting the Japanese out here at the time.

In the stories passed down to him, Bateri was told of his ancestors' fascination with how the Americans didn't have to work to get what they wanted. All the Americans had to do was scribble something on a piece of paper, wait a few days and then a flying machine would arrive and deliver whatever they desired. To this end, the Tannus wanted to be like the Americans, so they copied their close quarter drills, how they acted, how they dressed, even how they walked and talked.

But when the war was over the Americans went away, much to the Tannus' dismay. Trying to think of anything that would bring them back, Bateri's great-grandfather and his counselors espoused a religion around that very belief. They built models of the airplanes they'd seen, they constructed airstrips, they kept marching their close quarter drills, convinced these rituals would be noticed by the gods and compel them to return.

But they never did . . . until today.

That was only a part of the story, though.

When these new invaders first came to the islands almost six years ago, Bateri was captured along with nearly four thousand of the tribe's boys, women and men. They knew their captors only as Yellow Star, because just about everything they'd brought with them—from weapons to whips—had a tiny yellow star embossed on it. The Yellow Star soldiers wore distinct multi-colored combat suits and they also always wore masks—decorated ski masks, actually—in a place that frequently reached 100 degrees F before 10 AM.

While the women were used as sex slaves for the Yellow Star guards, the Tannu men and boys were brought to the next island over and forced to work inside the volcanic crater. On their backs, and for many, the loss of their own lives, the foundation for what would become the monstrous collection of mirrors was built.

As the months turned into years, and many of the Tannu men were worked to death, their bodies were disposed of on Death Pit Island. Whenever there was a shortage in the number of slaves, the Yellow Star would go to Vatu and take the strongest boys, and eventually the strongest women too. Anyone who was no use to them, such as the elderly and the sick, were executed on the spot.

No surprise, as taskmasters the YS invaders were beyond brutal. It became routine to shoot anyone they deemed not working hard enough, leaving the body there for all to see until it was thrown away with the others who'd succumbed to exhaustion or beatings or both.

Bateri himself worked on the mirrors for more than five years, counseling his people that they must stay alive, must keep working and keep praying that the gods would someday help them. One day, a guard felt Bateri wasn't working hard enough, so he hit him in the head with a gun butt. Broken and bloody, when the chief came to, he was on a boat with two dozen dead bodies, heading for Death Pit Island.

He was thrown into the shallow quarry, and there he lay atop a bundle of corpses for an entire day and night before a freak rainstorm gave him the opportunity to crawl out. Only slightly mad, he swam back to Vatu, a place he hadn't been to in years, even though he'd been just a few miles away all that time. What he found were the few remaining members of his once-burgeoning tribe. Everyone else was dead.

But as soon as he'd recovered from his injuries, Chief Bateri started going back up to the holy plateau. Fearing the Tannus would soon disappear completely, he would perform the old rituals every night and beseech the gods to return and save his people.

And now, incredibly, that had happened.

Chief Bateri stumbled into his hidden camp, so excited he nearly wet himself during the long run down from the holy plateau.

It was just after midnight and those in the village who saw him were confused at first. The chief never left his guard atop the plateau until dawn.

Unless . . .

They helped him to the center of the camp where the ceremonial tree drum was located. There was certain pattern he was supposed to play for this momentous event, but he'd forgotten it already. So he just started hammering away on the hollowed log as loud and as fast as he could.

Within thirty seconds, the rest of the villagers were gathered around him—all 22 of them. They were mostly elderly, some hobbled by permanent injuries, others just lucky not to have been captured by the Yellow Star in the first place.

Bateri was not a young man. It took him a few moments after banging the tree drum before he could address his tiny band of survivors. Finally collecting himself, he told them, lowly and slowly, a new god had come, in a different kind of flying machine.

The god told Bateri that with the Tannus' help, he and his fellow gods would try to oust the Yellow Star overlords. But the tribe would have to help save their brothers and sisters on Mirror Island first.

The villagers all had the same question: how could they, the feeble and the lame, possibly help the gods?

Bateri knew his answer would be puzzling, as it was when first told to him. But he believed the wisest thing they could do now was work with the gods and hope they could rescue their relatives and save their homeland.

So he asked his people to gather round.

Then he told them, "This is what they want us to do . . ."

Chapter Twenty-Two

Slugboat 7 reached its assigned position just at midnight, right on time.

Stopping a half mile off the northern tip of Mirror Island, they killed their engines and dropped anchor. It was a crystal clear night and the stars were brilliant, but luckily there was no moon.

They were running dark, in radio silence. Each one of the seven-man crew was at his battle station; Lieutenant Ruggeri was at the helm. They'd had just a couple hours to prep for this special mission and they were a long way from home, that being the USS *USA,* presently sailing figure eights, a hundred miles to the north.

It had been a long ride in, and it promised to be a long ride out.

If they made it that far.

Part of that hasty two-hour prep included instructions on what to do if the main mirror on the island, the truly gigantic four-sided one in the middle of the other twelve, was doing a "purge." That's what Club the weatherman had called it. The bright lights caused by the Yellow Star's bizarre sun-collecting gear were not only apparent during the day, but sometimes at night too, though these bursts were intermittent and unpredictable.

The theory was the main mirror had to purge it itself of any random electrical charges before starting anew the following day. This would cause a sudden, blinding, violent flash of light to erupt between the big mirror and the energy collector on Battery Island.

Should it occur, Slugboat 7's crew was told, just sit tight and don't let it get to you.

That was easier said than done as within one minute of their arrival, they witnessed a purging. It was like seeing a gigantic lightning bolt extremely up close and personal, no more than 100 feet away. The night lit up, there was an ear-splitting *crack!* and then, it was gone.

But the bolt's electromagnetic pulse was so severe, it knocked out the Slugboat's communication and navigation gear. Now they were really out here alone. Yet the most terrifying thing for the crew members was wondering if and when the lightning bolt was going to happen again.

There were six massive electrical discharges in the next thirty minutes. Each one was startling, loud and unsettling, nothing anyone could ever get used to. But Slugboat 7's crew stood fast.

Finally, out of the dark, another boat came into view. It was a long hollowed out canoe with an outrunner. Two men were rowing it very slowly; a third was up on the bow.

This man whistled, one note, three times. Ruggeri whistled back.

Their contact was here.

Ruggeri gave two hand signals to the portside gun crew. They disappeared below decks.

Another purging erupted, sending a tree trunk thick bolt of electricity almost directly over their heads. By the time the canoe had pulled alongside, the gun crew had re-appeared on deck.

As quickly and carefully as possible, they lowered a satchel the size of a large gunny sack over to the men in the canoe. Despite the high nighttime temperature, the sack was cold to the touch.

Putting on a flak jacket and an oversized Fritz helmet, Ruggeri shouldered his M-16 and climbed down into the canoe himself.

He looked up at his XO. "Remember—you wait here exactly one hour. If I'm not back by then, you leave. That's an order . . ."

The XO just looked back at him and gave him a mock salute.

"Sure thing, Captain . . ." he replied.

*****

Fifty-nine minutes went by.

Slugboat 7 stayed at its position, crew on battle stations, with no running lights, the engines shut down and the radio dead.

The stars might have been bright, but it was inky black down at the water's surface—except when the big mirror would light up their universe for two or three terrifying seconds.

The hour came and went. The armed tug stayed on station, every man's eyes trained on the northern coast of Mirror Island. They could see a dull glare over the top of the volcanic crater, signs of activity going on just inside. All it would take was for someone to see them by the light of a purge and they'd been dead ducks.

But they were not leaving without their CO.

Another ten minutes went by. Finally, they saw a bare light against the dark coast heading in their direction.

The XO ordered the Slugboat's engine turned back on and they started right for the light, just hoping it was a signal from the Tannu canoe. They got their answer when they saw Lt. Ruggeri standing on the bow of the canoe, looking angry and relieved at the same time.

The canoe pulled up to the tug. Ruggeri gave each of his new Tannu friends a salute. Then his XO helped him back onto the tug.

"Disobeying a direct order?" Ruggeri asked.

"That's correct, sir," the XO replied dryly.

"Well, for that—thank you very much," Ruggeri told him.

He waved to the Tannu canoe one last time and the two boats parted ways, heading in opposite directions.

Once Slugboat 7 was on its way, the XO asked Ruggeri: "Successful delivery, sir?"

The CO climbed out of his flak jacket and secured his M-16.

"Melted a little quicker than we thought," he replied. "But overall—mission accomplished."

Chapter Twenty-Three

Arizona

The hastily arranged convoy left Los Angeles at dawn the following morning. Traveling at speeds in excess of 90 mph, they were in Phoenix before noon.

There were five Humvees, all attached to the LA Army. Four were filled with armed soldiers. The fifth was carrying a team of electronic warfare technicians.

They turned onto Interstate 10 outside Phoenix and headed south. Maintaining their high speed, they were on the outskirts of Tucson thirty minutes later.

Off at East Valencia Road, then over to South Kolb, they were soon approaching what before the Big War was called Davis-Monthan Air Force Base. But it was better known then and now as The Boneyard.

This was where the old U.S. military sent its elderly warplanes to die. Hundreds of them had been stored here before the Big War. Since then, many had been cannibalized or just stolen and sold outright.

However, there were some aircraft still intact at the immense air base—and ironically the Americans had the AMC to thank for that. When they'd invaded the American west coast years before, the AMC's lines stretched all the way out here to the Boneyard. Even though they didn't have the technological know how on getting any of the planes back in the air, they'd sealed off the place and kept the thieves out for more than a decade.

The convoy pulled up to the Boneyard's main gate to find a vintage Lear business jet waiting on the other side. The plane was painted in bright yellow and blue, the colors of the Football City Armed Forces.

Two men from the plane greeted the first humvee. One was Louis St. Louis. Tall with a shock of white hair, he was a staunch patriot and mayor of Football City, formerly known as St. Louis, Missouri. The other man, shorter and older, was the infamous arms dealer, Roy From Troy.

After a brief conversation, they squeezed into the lead vehicle and led it to a section of the air base about a half mile away. The column sped between rows of elderly B-47 and B-58 bombers, C-5 cargo planes and retired KC-135 aerial tankers. Some of them had been butchered right down to the landing gear. Others were missing engines, cockpits, entire tail sections.

But when they reached the section labeled L7, they found an area roped off with old-fashioned yellow caution tape. Seven vintage airplanes were inside this cordoned-off area. Three were B-52H models, two were monstrous

C-5 cargo planes and two were KC-135 aerial tankers. Ten members of St Louis' personal bodyguard were watching over the odd collection of aircraft.

The LA Army soldiers from the humvees reinforced this guard, while the EW techs headed right for the trio of B-52s. Climbing into the cockpit of the first B-52, the techs unscrewed a panel next to the fuel consumption gauge on the lower left hand side, near the throttles. Behind this panel was the bomber's autopilot module. They disconnected it from the main power buss and examined the inputs on the bottom of the device. There were two main plugs, but there was also an auxiliary plug input available.

That's all the techs needed to see. One of them opened the bomber's cockpit window and got St. Louis's attention below. He held up three fingers and then gave him a thumbs up.

St. Louis clenched his fist in triumph. It hadn't been a wasted trip.

He turned to Roy From Troy. "You've been involved in a million of these things," he said. "How crazy is this idea?"

The little old guy just laughed.

"Nothing even comes close," he replied. "This is the nuttiest one yet."

Over the next hour, he and St. Louis checked over the other planes in the cordoned off area. Roy was the expert. He pronounced all of them airworthy.

"Change the oil," he said. "And they should be good to go."

An hour later, St. Louis and Roy were out on the base's main runway.

It was now close to sunset. They were both watching the time.

Finally . . .

Off to the west, still far away but getting closer, a mechanical rumbling that transformed into a roar and then into a scream all in a matter of seconds. Coming directly at them, appearing out of the setting sun, was a Su-34 VLR fighter from the United American Naval Air Force.

"He's always a little late," St. Louis said dryly.

"But never by much," Roy responded

The huge attack fighter landed and taxied up to them. The under fuselage access door opened and two men climbed out. One was Tony 3, looking a little pale.

The other was Hawk Hunter.

They all shook hands. They were all old friends.

Then St. Louis told him the words he wanted to hear. "The Buffs' autopilots have auxiliary plug-ins."

A look of relief washed over Hunter's face. But it was quickly replaced by one of concern.

"So, we're going to try this then?" he asked them.

St. Louis nodded.

"Looks like you've got all the gear you need," he told Hunter. "If your gizmo works, then we'll load them up and everything will be green on this end."

Hunter looked at Tony, nearly recovered from their high-altitude, high-speed dash across the Pacific. The filmmaker just shrugged.

"Only one way to find out . . ." he said.

The night passed with some frenetic activity at the base. The three B-52s were loaded with 70,000 pounds of bombs in their weapons bays, plus their interiors were packed with crates of dynamite and barrels of gasoline. All this, flown out just a few hours earlier, courtesy of Roy From Troy.

The two C-5 giants were fueled up and given extra drop tanks under their wings. The pair of KC-135 tankers was also gassed, as was the navalized Su-34.

A much larger convoy arrived at the base around midnight. Twenty-five troop trucks in all, they were carrying 1,000 LA Army soldiers plus their weapons and gear. They were processed and then put inside the pair of Galaxy cargo behemoths.

By dawn, they were almost ready to go.

At precisely 0600 hours—just as the sun was coming up—there was another loud roar over the base. Coming out of the morning mist of the east was a dozen F-20 Tigersharks from the Football City Air Corps. They too were carrying large external fuel tanks, as well as an array of weapons beneath their wings.

The F-20s, unmistakable in their vivid Tigershark yellow and orange camouflage schemes, went into a slow orbit around the Boneyard as the small air fleet below lined up on the base's main runway.

They took off, one by one, the B-52s first, then the C-5s, then the tankers and the Su-34.

The big planes formed up high overhead, and then as one, and with the F-20s riding shotgun, turned west and headed back towards the Pacific.

Chapter Twenty-Four

There was no morgue on Mirror Island.

There'd never been a need for one. The brutal conditions under which the sun-stealing operation worked resulted in about a dozen slaves dying each day, either from exhaustion or a beating. But their remains would eventually be thrown onto a garbage scowl for the daily trip over to Death Pit Island, where they were dumped and burned.

It was an efficient way to dispose of the trash—but now, not having a morgue presented an unexpected crisis for Colonel Ding Toon, the Yellow Star commander on Mirror Island. Short, wiry and perpetually on opioids, he needed to examine a body in absolute secrecy. But with no mortuary and no place really secure on the island, he wound up doing it in his bedroom.

That's where the corpse in question was right now. Battered, bloody and leaking, it was laying on a rug on the floor next to his bed.

Toon was there with three others: the camp's medical officer, the captain of the island's guard and a platoon leader known only by the number 12866. Like everyone in Yellow Star, they were all wearing stylized ski masks which hid their features 24/7, even while sleeping. Toon's mask showed a smiling ghoul with vampire teeth, something from a very bad dream. Because of their lower rank, the others' masks weren't as graphic.

The bedroom itself was a strange place. The walls were adorned with shrunken heads, scalps and bizarre death masks. Weeping witches, ghostly figures with no eyes. Devils with toothless grins. The room was lit only by candles, some burning away inside human skulls. So a dead body here might not have seemed all that unusual.

But this corpse presented a big problem for Colonel Toon for one overwhelming reason: it was wearing the unmistakable black, red and orange officer's uniform of the Asian Mercenary Cult.

Walking a picket duty, 12866 had found the body partially buried in the sand in a small cove on the northern end of the island. There was no question it was an AMC officer. No other armed forces in the world wore black, red and orange as their colors—no one wanted to. But the uniform and the person wearing it posed a major puzzle for Toon and the Yellow Star. Their drones had attacked the AMC fleet in mid-Pacific because no one in Asia, least of all them, wanted a rival army of murderers and rapists running loose along the Pacific Rim. It had been just easier to kill them all—and let people around the globe know just what the Yellow Star could do.

But that attack had happened thousands of miles from here, and their photo reconnaissance drones had indicated every last one of the AMC soldiers had been killed in some way or other.

Yet the body on the floor seemed to be proof this wasn't the case. When found, the dead AMC officer had a valise chained to its left wrist. Inside was a packet of documents written in both English and Mandarin that contained the equivalent of a nuclear bombshell for the Yellow Star.

Not all the AMC soldiers perished in the ocean massacre; the documents spelled this out in great detail. A large number of the cultists had survived somehow, had regrouped and, incredibly, were planning to invade the YS's Solomon Island bases in retaliation.

It was all there: maps, weather reports, troop strengths and tactical contingencies for a simultaneous five-prong amphibious assault on both Battery and Mirror Islands. The operation was so detailed, the beaches the AMC planned to attack on both islands had been given code names: Omaha, Utah, Juno, Sword and Gold.

But the real shocker involved where this attack would be coming from: Death Pit Island. The plans contained lists of AMC soldiers who had already infiltrated onto the island, landing under the cover of darkness and, after bribing the YS guards running the crater crematorium, had stayed quiet and hidden. These lists were so detailed, they even included how many pieces of silver each YS turncoat was paid to keep their mouth shut.

On the plan's last page was the most incredible piece of intelligence of all: the twin invasions were set to launch at dawn the following morning.

Colonel Toon was in a quandary, an unusual situation for him. Created in the city of Wuhan, China, as a post-war low-cost merc outfit, Yellow Star had grown into a conquering army so quickly, its fighting forces had only performed offensive military operations. Invade and occupy, that's what they did. Toon really didn't know how to defend anything, never mind Battery and Mirror Islands.

But he had to do something.

So, he ordered the 1,500 troops on Mirror Island to get ready for a defensive operation, details to follow.

Chapter Twenty-Five

It was a quiet morning on Disney Island.

The waves lapped against the shorelines all around the perfectly shaped landmass. A mist was forming above the wave tops. Everything had a hazy look.

But at exactly 0700 hours, the tranquility was broken by the sound of a dull mechanical growl. Airplanes were approaching from the east.

Antiaircraft sites all over the island began lighting up. Radar dishes turned on, twelve substantial blips popping up on their acquisition screens. That was a lot of aerial traffic coming their way. But it was way up at 42,000 feet—eight miles high.

Two minutes went by. The bogies drew closer. The island's extensive AA network was burning red hot by now. The dozen high flying airplanes were only a minute away from being directly over the island.

The question was: who were they?

The island's AA system could not answer that. The only thing the network's electronic brain could confirm was that no YS aircraft were scheduled to arrive on Disney Island this morning.

So, these aircraft did not belong to them.

The system sent out a command for all AA weapons to arm and get ready. Seconds later, the contrails of twelve approaching aircraft came into view. They were not answering the YS radio commands to identify themselves. The next step in the system was to fire on them.

A barrage of SA-2 SAM missiles launched a moment later. They ascended from different parts of the island, going almost straight up, roaring to 42,000 feet. Even though the missiles were traveling at more than the speed of sound, it would take a few crucial seconds for them to reach their targets.

So, all eyes, electronic and otherwise, were fixed skyward at that moment, waiting to see what was going to happen.

It was a classic misdirection. While all the attention was upwards, eight miles over the island, there was suddenly another huge roar, this one much, much closer—and lower.

Flying out of the morning came three enormous dark shapes. There were no more than 500 feet off the ground and the noise preceding them was thunderous.

They were the three B-52s resurrected from the Boneyard. They came over the island one at a time, in a staggered-line formation, making so much noise, anyone on the ground who heard them could suddenly hear nothing else. At the same moment, the SAM missiles fired at the high altitude aircraft either exploded harmlessly or had gone wildly off course, their intended targets executing a brilliant last-second backwards-flower fall-away flip maneuver that served to confuse the radar guidance systems of all the SA-2s.

The lead B-52 roared over the island unmolested, quickly disappearing into the morning fog. The second Stratofortress was right on its tail, followed by the third plane of the trio.

But at the last instant, this B-52 suddenly veered off course. Turning on its left wing, its tip hit the ground, sending the huge bomber cartwheeling into the side of the island's mountain.

It exploded like a small atom bomb, collapsing the north end of the peak and vaporizing part of the huge steel door leading into the hidden hangar.

Chapter Twenty-Six

The Yellow Star soldier known only as 12866 couldn't believe his luck.

In a military hierarchy where any kind of advancement was nearly impossible, by his good fortune of finding the dead AMC officer's body, he'd been field-promoted to lieutenant and elevated out of the guard force and into a combat unit.

The downside was he was going into combat right away.

That body, and the documents it was carrying, had turned the Yellow Star post on Mirror Island upside down. Prior to this, any YS soldiers assigned to the island were used strictly as guards. Their job was to control the thousands of native slaves needed to make the sunlight farming operation work. Almost none of them had ever been in actual combat.

But now, with Commander Toon convinced their piece of the Solomon Islands was about to be invaded by the AMC, almost the entire 1500-man guard force had been hastily converted into combat troops. At the moment, they were all en route to Death Pit Island to do battle with the cult's infiltrators and to seek out and execute the turncoats who'd allowed them to hide there.

12866 was both excited and nervous. Like most of them he'd never been in combat before either. He'd joined Yellow Star just to get out of his tiny village in western China. He thought he was going to see the world and make some silver, but it hadn't turned out that way. At least not yet.

There were more than a thousand newly minted infantry troops loaded into the ten barges usually used to move supplies and bodies between the islands. 12866 and his newly assigned combat company were on the last barge to leave Mirror Island for the five mile open water journey to the Death Pit.

This put him in a perfect position to see what happened next.

It was 0715 hours; the morning sun was up and getting hot. Eight of the barges had already reached the Death Pit and were storming the island. 12866's vessel was about ten minutes away from landing.

Suddenly everyone on his barge heard a tremendously loud deep groan even over the racket their engine was making. They all looked east to see a large airplane flying low over the water and heading right for them.

At first they thought it was the double-747 Mothership—the aerial command center for the Yellow Star's vast air fleet of drones. Though stationed on an island some distance away, the huge airplane was seen occasionally in the skies over Mirror Island.

The soldiers on the barge let out a cheer. They were certain this was the Mothership and its drone force here to do battle against the AMC troops hidden on Death Pit Island.

But as the seconds went by, it became obvious the cheering had been premature. This was not the steroidal 747. It was almost as big, but it was painted in a menacing dark gray, was flying very low and slow and leaving eight dirty smoke trails in its wake.

Another officer on 12866's barge studied the aircraft with his binoculars; he nearly dropped the spy glasses when he realized what he was looking at. The airplane was a B-52 heavy bomber, possibly the most famous warplane the United States ever built. They were a rare item in the postwar world—yet now one of them, wearing the colors of the U.S. Air Force, was coming right at them.

It went overhead two seconds later—at just 500 feet off the water, the roar of its eight engines was earsplitting. Creatures of reflex, everyone on the barge ducked. When they were able to see the big plane again, it had begun a low slow turn around the opposite side of Death Pit Island.

By this time, the bulk of the YS troops on the island were in the process of climbing up the side of the ancient volcano, anxious to secure the high ground for the battle ahead. They'd spotted the B-52 by now, realized what it was and had opened fire on it. But the hurriedly assembled invasion force did not bring any portable antiaircraft weapons with them. And while both Battery Island and Mirror Island were thick with AA sites, there had never been a need for them on Death Pit Island because it was basically a cemetery.

A storm of tracer fire rose up from the side of the crater, all of it fired at the circling B-52. The fusillade looked dramatic in the early morning sun, but it had no effect on the huge bomber. It completed its turn, went to full power—and slammed into the side of the crater right where the YS armed force was advancing upwards.

It hit with such force, and caused such an explosion, a small mushroom cloud rose above the island. The roar of the blast quickly faded away and, save for the crackling of flames which now covered nearly half the island, all was suddenly quiet.

For about five seconds.

Then suddenly another B-52 flew right over their heads, just as loud, just as low, just as frightening.

But this one was heading for Battery Island.

Chapter Twenty-Seven

Good things came in threes—or at least that's what Hawk Hunter was hoping for this morning.

His plan was unfolding pretty much on time, which was important because every element had to happen almost precisely if it was all going to work.

The Tony Fix, as it had become known, was as simple as could be imagined. By connecting a small radio receiver to the B-52's autopilot's auxiliary plug, Tony had basically recreated the guidance system of the crashed Yellow Star drone, right down to using a pocket calculator for power and computing.

The fix allowed Tony to control the autopilots on all three B-52s—in effect, he turned them into drones. Not crappy little bomb carriers with lawn mower engines. These were postwar American-style drones. Gigantic, capable of carrying 70,000 pounds of bombs, plus another 10,000 pounds of explosives packed inside, fly one into its target at 500 knots and it will definitely light things up like a little nuke.

The blast, the noise and the destruction—it will all look frighteningly familiar, if you lived to tell about it.

One downside of this was Tony 3—the brains of the operation, but who hated flying—had been doing a lot of it lately. The supersonic sprint in the Su-34 across the Pacific to the Boneyard; the ride back in the lead B-52, sub-sonic, very bumpy.

Their plane—Buff 1—was a little different. It had been partially turned into the UA's equivalent of the Jumbo-Jumbo. From here, by communicating via radio with the autopilots in each one, Tony was able to fly Buff 2 and Buff 3 and help them complete their missions: punching a hole in the impregnable entrance to the mountain fortress on Disney Island, as well as destroying all the vileness that was Death Pit Island.

But as Hunter said more than once on this ride over, "Now, comes the fun part . . ."

Because now came the most crucial element of all: he had to bail out of the B-52 he was piloting at the moment. Strapped in beside him, still a bit pale from all they'd done and what they had to do, was Tony 3. He would have to bail out too.

They were now nearly a minute out from Battery Island—and they had to do the next three things very quickly.

First, Hunter had to turn over command of the airplane to the autopilot; then Tony had to open up a channel to start sending radio signals to his fix-it inside the autopilot. This could take a few seconds. Or longer.

Hunter would have to hold the plane steady and on its gradual downward course until then, which was getting increasingly more difficult as they were now picking up AA fire from Battery Island. Then, they had to arm the bombs in the bomb bay and fuse the high explosives packed from the navigator's station to the tail end of the airplane.

Only then could they hit the silk.

They had practiced this drill many times to kill the hours over the dark Pacific—but that had been without AA fire, which was now a torrent. And, of course, without a real bail out, which Tony 3 was particularly dreading.

At one point he'd said to Hunter: "It's different for you. You do this kind of stuff all the time."

To which Hunter had replied: "No, I don't. *This* is nuts . . ."

They reached the magic one minute mark and Hunter punched two buttons on his autopilot. Three painful seconds went by. Four . . . five . . . They were at 400 feet and plunging fast. The dead square shape of the huge electric storage unit quickly filling their cockpit wind screen.

Finally, the green light began blinking in Tony's radio control set. He flipped a switch and the B-52's death plunge was now on autopilot.

Hunter quickly armed the 70,000 pounds of bombs in the plane's bomb bay, while Tony connected the fuses for the packed HE to a pair of leads on a small car battery. Now they were going somewhere—the next fifty or so seconds would tell exactly where.

They were both wearing the parachutes, but this was not going to be an ejection. The B-52 threw ejecting pilots out of a stricken craft with such violence, it could affect the speed and more importantly the course of the huge bomber.

So, this was in fact a bail out. They both hurried down to the bottom tier of the jet where Hunter used his boot to kick open the under-fuselage access panel. The first thing they saw of the outside world was an SA-7 portable anti-aircraft missile streaking by not twenty feet away.

Tony looked at Hunter. The plane was less than 300 feet from plowing in. As calmly as possible, Hunter said to him, "It's time to go, remember to pull the cord."

Then he pushed Tony through the hole, an act that took a moment to complete as the filmmaker needed a quick squeeze to get out.

Hunter was right behind him.

Both their chutes opened, but like any airdrop, it looked to Hunter like the rest of the world was moving crazily and he was hanging dead still. The tracer fire coming up at them was thick enough to run across, and every few moments, they'd hear a huge whooshing sound and another SAM missile would shoot by them.

Hunter saw the B-52 get hit many, many times on its way down. The AA shells tore into the vintage airplane mercilessly—but it didn't matter. The old warhorse never wavered from its mission. It slammed into the giant battery with such force, a shock wave made up of mini lightning bolts shot out of it from every direction, turning quickly into neon aura.

They both saw it all on the way down.

And despite the commotion and the ordnance still flying around them, Hunter still heard Tony 3 cry out: *"There's your fucking drones!"*

Chapter Twenty-Eight

There had been deep concern that the attack on Disney Island would be costly for the United Americans.

It was their first target in this hastily assembled island-hopping campaign and essential if the plan was going to work. Because they not only had to deliver the first bomb-laden B-52 drone to the right spot, they had to follow that up with what was probably the most dangerous military mission in the book: the air landing assault.

This wasn't dropping paratroopers over the island. This was slam-landing the two C-5s and hoping the LA Army soldiers inside were able to get out in good condition, do battle and, in theory, take over the island.

The biggest problem was the UA had almost zero intelligence on the place they were invading. But there was no other way to do it. That's why every soldier in the LA Army landing party was a volunteer.

At just about the same moment the B-52 drone hit the side of the mountain fortress, the two C-5 Galaxy cargo planes banged down at the far end of the southernmost ten-mile long double runway. Flying barely 1,000 feet off the ground, JT Toomey's Su-34 squadron cleared a path in front of the two enormous cargo planes. Anything that moved anywhere near the runway was blasted by the Su-34s' twin nose cannons.

Meanwhile the two C-5s kept rolling down the runway—this was part of the plan. Gunfire erupted from all sides, following the two giant planes down the ultra-long double airstrip. But anytime a weapon would zero in on the C-5s, one of the Americanized Su-34s would swoop down and take it out.

It took the two C-5s almost five minutes to run this gauntlet, but finally they reached the northern end of the runway, where they stopped. They were only taking scattered fire at this point, so the rear doors of the big planes opened and LA Army soldiers came pouring out, ready for the gun battle of their lives.

And that's what they got, but not in any way they could have expected.

Those first troopers out of the huge planes came face to face with a large force of the island's defenders, oddly camouflaged in yellow and green-striped combat uniforms and wearing the tropical version of ski masks. They had been lying in wait in the sea grass that bordered the massive runway.

They began firing as soon as the first LA Army soldiers appeared—but they were shooting wildly and not with any accuracy. There had to be at least five hundred gunmen on both sides of the runway, with another group directly in front of them, close to the still burning wreckage of the B-52. With any kind of tactics, the enemy could easily surround the two C-5s. Should that happen, the UA's contingency plan was a near suicidal drill of everyone getting back into the giant planes, turning them around and flying off the island.

But everyone knew the chances of that succeeding were basically zero. That's why what happened next was so bizarre.

The enemy gunmen were suddenly reinforced. At least another *thousand* of the oddly attired soldiers jumped up from the sea grass just a few hundred feet behind the first wave, and they too began firing on the two airplanes. But just as before, none of it was anywhere near accurate. It was as if the defenders were firing their weapons for the first time.

This all took place in less than fifteen seconds and miraculously none of LA Army soldiers had been killed—yet. But there was so much ordnance flying around, it was only a matter of time before something big hit one of the C-5s and that would be the ballgame. If either of the airplanes could not fly, it would be impossible for all of the troopers to get on the remaining plane and get out. That would trigger Plan C: All of the carrier's helicopters were standing by for an emergency extraction.

But again, everyone knew that had valiant disaster written all over it.

But just as it looked like some kind of retreat was going to be the only option, the enemy gunmen suddenly started falling over. Just a few at first, but then like dominoes they all began dropping around the stunned LA Army troops.

It looked like they were being shot—but the Americans had stopped firing by this point. Still, within ten seconds, all of the enemy soldiers were down.

This didn't make sense. The Football City F-20s playing the part of the high-altitude attack ruse were still orbiting overhead, eight miles up. JT's Su-34s were circling the island at 1,000 feet, firing on any weapons emplacement they could find, but knowing enough to stay clear of any action on the ground until they were called in for support.

So, it wasn't anyone on the American side that had dispatched the hundreds of enemy troops.

The Americans froze in place, not quite sure what to do. There was no more small-arms fire. And, no more fire from weapons on the side of the mountain. Everything had taken place in less than a minute—an eternity in combat, but quick in real time.

Finally, a few of the LA troops ventured out of their cover and approached the field of fallen troops. There were rings of them all around the C-5s; it was scary for the Americans to see just how close they'd come from being overrun.

The first gunmen they came to were clustered around the front wheel of the number one C-5. There were five of them and the troopers took precautions to kick their weapons away before examining the enemy gunmen themselves.

They weren't shot—at least this group wasn't. They couldn't see any violence to their bodies at all. But they were certainly dead.

They removed a mask from one of the enemy soldiers. The man was Asian, probably mid-20s and had a blank almost peaceful expression on his face. One LA soldier noticed something sticking out of the gunman's collar. It was a silver wire about a six inches long. Further investigation found that it was attached to a small device the size of a postage stamp that had been imbedded in the skin of the man's neck. It had two tiny lights, but only one was on. It was red and blinking.

"Lost signal?" one trooper asked the other.

When they found similar devices on the others nearby, they called back for their unit's communications engineer. This man ran and up and studied the devices. It took him nearly a minute; by that time, a deathly quiet had fallen over the entire island.

Finally, the engineer could only hazard a guess—and it was a wild one.

"Some kind of signals transmitter, sending impulses to the brain, maybe?" he said.

"Making them . . .?" one trooper asked.

The engineer just shrugged. "If someone was somehow giving them orders through this thing—and they're obeying? Then I guess you could call them human robots. Or zombies. Take your pick."

He started to leave when the trooper asked him: "But *why* did they die?"

The engineer shrugged again. "I'd say whatever was sending those signals ran out of juice. A power blackout would do it . . ."

Then he finally scrambled away.

The LA Army soldiers uneasily looked at the hundreds of deceased YS soldiers all around them. It was just so weird.

Finally, one of the soldiers said: "If any of these guys start coming back to life, I'm swimming home."

Chapter Twenty-Nine

Hunter and Tony had hit the water at just about the same time, two big splashes in the bright-blue morning Pacific.

Debris from what they had just done rained down on them. Everything from pieces of the B-52 to whole palm trees. Secondary explosions were rocking the island, causing mini-tidal waves of surface debris to batter them as they untangled themselves from their parachutes.

The water around them was catching fire. With a great crash, the remains of the battery station collapsed in on itself, causing even brighter neon bolts of electricity to go streaking across the already-fiery sky.

This was clearly no place to be.

Fortunately, they wouldn't be here long.

Just moments after getting out of their chutes, they heard the welcoming sound of a large maritime engine. A few seconds later, Slugboat 7 appeared out of the smoke and mist. It was their ride out of hell.

The starboard-side gun crew hauled them aboard. Once they were safely on deck, someone buried the throttles and the armed tugboat took off. They were soon traveling at twenty-five knots, heading dead east, out of the cauldron.

Lieutenant Ruggeri climbed down from the steering house and hastily shook hands with them.

"Goddamn, finally this thing is over," Tony said in triumph.

But the look on Ruggeri's face said something different.

"I'm sorry, guys," was how he started. "But we've got a glitch . . ."

Hunter's shoulders sagged immediately.

"Mirror Island?" he asked.

Ruggeri nodded glumly.

"I guess it's a real mess over there," he said.

JAWS CO Jim Cook could attest to that.

How to attack Mirror Island had been the most challenging part of the UA's hastily assembled island-hopping plan.

There were more than three thousand Tannu slaves inside the crater. They had to be out of harm's way before the carrier's Su-34 squadrons bombed the place to dust.

So, the plan had called for the JAWS and NJ104 special forces' units to land on the island and start climbing as soon as they saw Battery Island blow up.

Recon by a high-flying Su-34 earlier that morning showed the ruse of the dead AMC officer had worked. Many of the island's guards had been sent on the dead-end mission to Death Pit Island, leaving behind a skeleton force, later learned to be about a hundred men. Upon reaching the top of the crater, the plan called for the American Special Forces teams to engage the remaining YS soldiers and keep them at bay until the Tannu slaves realized they were free—and then, possibly, finish off the YS soldiers themselves.

But about halfway up to the side of the crater, Cook and his men received the strange report about the fighting on Disney Island. The UA had triumphed there, but only because all the Yellow Star defenders suddenly dropped dead before any kind of battle ever began. LA Army medics speculated the bombing of Battery Island created a surge of electrical impulses coming from radio-controlled devices implanted in the YS soldiers' skin, causing their brains to literally short circuit, killing them instantly.

It almost sounded too weird, but on arriving at the crater's lip, the UA special forces teams saw the same thing had happened here: many of the guards remaining on Mirror Island had also dropped dead.

Many, but not all.

As it turned out, two dozen of the island's defenders, mostly YS officers, somehow got smart real quick and pulled out their implants before they could kill them.

These survivors had taken refuge inside their large thatched-roof HQ located dead center of the crater. Painted in bright purple and red, it almost looked like a circus carousel.

At the southern end of the huge crater at least three thousand Tannu natives were jammed in behind the giant gear works building. They'd been using it as cover ever since they witnessed the YS suddenly dropping dead at their feet, something that caused mass confusion inside the crater.

And that was just the beginning.

Peering down from their positions on the lip of the crater—JAWS team in the middle, NJ104 watching the flanks—the special operators found the inside of the crater was now a scene of utter chaos.

It looked like the set for a sci-fi movie, one whose plot showed the world in a very twisted dystopian future. It was a small almost futuristic city for sure, but the forest of towering mirrors was just otherworldly. Ultra-gleaming and almost crystalline at their very tops, at their bottoms was the near-prehistoric machinery that actually turned the goliaths. Huge wooden gears, huge metal spokes, huge rubberized wheels—and miles and miles of bloody rope.

In the midst of all this, there was gunfire, people yelling over the PA system, fires everywhere. When the

Americans arrived, they saw about a hundred or so freed slaves running through the complex, intent on taking bloody revenge on those guards who never made it to the safety of the YS carnival-colored circular HQ.

These Tannu warriors were pummeling their bodies with anything they could get their hands on—years of bent up anger at their degradation finally exploding in mad rage. But it was to no good end because most of the guards were already dead, having fallen minutes before when the juice went out.

The Tannus stuck at the southern end of the crater had begun ceremonial drumming, rhythmically banging on trees, rocks, the side of the huge gear works itself—anything that made a noise if you hit it. It was their way of beseeching the gods to help them.

In the middle of this weird savagery was the Yellow Star command hut, now reinforced like a small fort. The huge conical loudspeaker on its roof was playing what only could have been a Yellow Star fight song. Added to the Tannus drumming it created a bizarre percussive soundtrack to the scene.

All this the American units saw just within the thirty seconds of their arrival. Like one of Dante's levels of Hell, Jim Cook would later write. It was a miniature world consumed by madness.

Still the Americans stuck to the plan. It called for the UA troops to engage the YS soldiers on arrival, so the Americans immediately opened up on the multi-colored HQ. But in one of their weirdest moments of a very weird battle, at that very same instant, the YS troops inside the HQ inexplicably began firing at the huge gear works building behind which many of the Tannu had taken refuge. But some of these freed slaves were armed too, having taken weapons from their former captors. As soon as the UA units opened up on the YS, and the YS had started firing on the Tannus, the Tannus just started firing back at everybody.

Suddenly a three-way gun battle was happening. Suddenly, a blizzard of ordnance was crisscrossing the crater; the tracer bullets alone blotted out the sun.

In the midst of this triple barrage, six of the huge mirrors were hit and blown to bits.

There had been neon lightning bolts over Battery Island and a mushroom cloud over the Death Pit. But at that moment, it looked like the ancient volcano on Mirror Island had blown its stack. Hit by the crazy three-sided fusillade, the six towers fell inwards, crashing into the center of the crater, causing an eruption of dirty white smoke and dust to shoot upwards, carrying millions of bits of reflective mirror glass with them.

Covering the island, this cloud dropped millions of these shards onto the jungle below. It looked like it was raining diamonds.

The three-way gun battle abruptly stopped the moment the mirrors came crashing to the ground, members of all three sides shocked at seeing the grand structures fall.

But after only thirty seconds of silence, tops, the Yellow Star holdouts inside the thatched HQ took a very bizarre tact. Cranking up the camp's PA system once again, they directed their message to the 3,000 former slaves and began broadcasting, of all things, an offer to form an alliance with them.

The YS officer making the announcement said the people at the northern end of the crater actually belonged to the Asian Mercenary Cult and that they were invading the island. The YS holdouts urged the Tannus to look at the smoke and fire coming from the other islands nearby as proof the AMC was here. The YS officers beseeched the Tannus, saying if they linked up, together they could drive the invaders back into the sea.

Therein lay the glitch; the UA's clever dead-man ruse had suddenly come back to bite them on the ass. Many of the Tannus had been on the island prison for almost five years; they had no idea what was going on around them. But they knew one thing: As bad as the Yellow Star was, the AMC was worse. They were psychopaths, murderers and rapists. Rumors said they ate cooked children for field rations.

And that was the present situation on the island. All the firing had died down, but the strange three-sided standoff had caused everything inside the crater to freeze.

This was the report as told by Cook to Dozer on the carrier and then to Lt. Ruggeri on Slugboat 7 and now to Hunter and Tony. He ended by emphasizing that Mirror Island was nowhere near being evacuated.

"But that's not good," Hunter said. "The guys are going to carpet bomb that place in . . ."

He looked to his wrist as if he had a watch there. Truth was, he'd never worn a watch in his life. He always knew what time it was.

Except at that exact moment.

"In thirty minutes," Ruggeri answered for him.

Once their lightning-quick island-hopping campaign was complete, the UA knew the wise thing to do was withdraw from the area as quickly as possible.

But if they didn't destroy Mirror Island, the job wouldn't be finished. Calling off the air strike would mean they'd have to go back to LA, get resupplied, and then come all the way back out here—and try it again.

No one wanted to do that.

It was Jim Cook and Clancy Miller of the JAWS team who came up with a possible solution. They shared it with the carrier, who then radioed it to Slugboat 7. It was simple: if the UA could get someone to convince the Tannu slaves whose side they should be on, that might end the impasse.

But they didn't have much time to do it.

Just seconds after Ruggeri finished explaining the situation to Hunter and Tony 3, they all heard the sound of an approaching helicopter. It was one of the Ka-27s from the carrier, the same type Hunter had piloted to the top of the holy plateau to start this whole plan in motion. That was barely two days ago, but it seemed more like a million years.

Hunter climbed to the roof of Slugboat 7's wheelhouse and caught onto the ladder thrown down by the Ka-27's crew. It took a really lucky and well-timed leap to catch on to the last rung and climb up.

As he was pulled aboard by the helo crew, he looked back down at Slugboat 7 to see Tony 3 on the deck, battered, disheveled and soaking wet, looking up smiling and saluting him.

Hunter saluted back.

*****

The helo dashed over to Tatu Island, coming down for a quick landing atop the holy plateau.

Twenty-three people were waiting for it. They were all holding burning torches.

Hunter spotted Chief Bateri in the small crowd. He was in full ceremonial garb. His people led him over to the helicopter where Hunter met him at the open side door. They greeted each other as old friends.

But the chief looked very nervous.

"I am afraid to do this," he whispered urgently to Hunter in broken English.

"Fly, you mean?" Hunter asked, strapping him into the copter.

"No," the chief replied. "I'm afraid if I fly away and become a god, I'll never see my people again."

Hunter almost laughed.

"Don't worry," he told him as the copter lifted off. "If we pull this off, you'll be better than a god to them. You'll be a hero."

Chapter Thirty

The helo arrived just in time.

The YS holdouts had just begun issuing thinly veiled do or die ultimatums to the Tannus to help them fight the AMC invaders—or else.

The copter orbited the crater twice at full throttle, flying about 1,000 feet up, out of reach of most small arms fire and quickly getting everyone's attention.

Cook, JAWS and NJ104 took their cue and opened up on the YS HQ, once again battering it with suppressive fire. Though there was no return fire, they kept up the fusillade until the Ka-27 landed on the opposite tip of the crater.

The helo kept its arc lights on. Even though it wasn't even noon, the smoke and the mist had made it hard to see until now. The UA special units kept up their barrage long enough for Bateri and Hunter to step out of the copter and into the spotlight.

That's when a sudden hush came over the crater. The UA teams ceased firing. The YS loudspeaker went quiet; followed by a series of muffled gunshots coming from within the thatched HQ, the YS troops finally taking the easy way out.

But the freed slaves hardly noticed. They were too enthralled by seeing their chief for the first time in many years.

One of the Ka-27 crewmen handed Bateri a microphone and turned on the copter's small PA system, which squealed with feedback for several long seconds. Finally, the electronics settled down and Bateri was able to speak. Making the most of the moment, and in broken English, he told the freed slaves that the men at the other end of the island were friends of the Tannus.

In fact, they were sent here by the gods to help them.

"And this person here, is the god we have been waiting for," he finished, completely stunning Hunter. "He's the one who came back to save us. He and his friends. His name is Hawk Fromm . . ."

He handed the microphone to Hunter just as, to the Wingman's utter amazement, the freed slaves began bowing and chanting his new name.

It lasted for about three seconds before he moved to put a stop to it.

Putting the microphone to his lips, he turned to Bateri and said: "My old friend, please tell them: I'm not a god. I'm just an American . . ."

PART FOUR

The Game of Drones

Chapter Thirty-One

Louie St. Louis, mayor of Football City and commander-in-chief of its armed forces, arrived on Disney Island with the first wave of troops. Roy From Troy, weapons dealer extraordinaire, came in with him.

They were almost eyewitnesses to the bizarre battle that followed the bang-in. The clash had happened so quickly, all the gunfire had stopped by the time they got off their C-5. They saw the bodies of the YS soldiers along the runways and clustered around the UA aircraft. Faces still masked, they were lying about as if they'd all just fallen asleep.

Both St. Louis and Roy had seen their share of battlefields over the years, but nothing like this.

"More Jonestown than Disneyland," Roy had said.

The American landing teams split in two. Soldiers from the first C-5 would advance towards the mountain fortress, where the remains of the B-52 drone were still burning brightly. Wearing an oversized Fritz helmet and carrying an M-16, Roy went with them.

When soldiers from the second C-5 were assigned to check the island's mountain for enemy activity, St. Louis asked to go along. Climbing into the lead humvee with two LA Army field commanders, they led a small convoy across the expansive runways and up the mountain road, all the while looking for any signs of bad guys.

What they found instead were the rows of bombed-out antiaircraft sites destroyed by the carrier's Su-34s and Football City's F-20 strike planes. At least three dozen individual debris fields dotted the side of the mountain. The flattened remains of AA guns and SAM sites, a few were still in flames.

But something was missing.

St Louis' humvee pulled over about halfway up the 1500-foot mountain, so he could get a closer look at one of the bombed-out SAM sites. This one was right next to the road and had taken a direct hit from a Shrike missile. There was nothing left except lots of burnt rubber and twisted metal.

That was the problem. There were no bodies. No dead AA crewmen killed in the airstrikes; no drink-the-Kool-Aid YS soldiers.

How did the AA site work? The nearby remains of an automatic acquisition and targeting module provided the clue. These components allowed an AA site to be programmed to fire automatically, with no humans involved.

Realizing this, St. Louis felt his stomach do a flip.

This was not good . . .

He got back into the humvee and resumed the drive up the mountain.

They saw more of the same along the way. Lots of destroyed hardware. Lots of evidence of pinpoint air strikes. But no bodies.

Reaching the summit, they came upon one Yellow Star structure that had somehow survived the furious bombing. Standing alone on a ledge near the mountain's peak, it was no more than a shack with an antenna dish and a grounding pole next to it. A sign on the door identified it as an auxiliary radar data collection unit. It too looked unmanned.

As the rest of the American convoy arrived and established their position at the top of the mountain, St. Louis told the field commanders he'd like to examine the untouched hut. Two soldiers climbed up to the ledge with him, but he went inside the shack himself.

Fifteen seconds later, he came out, staggering a bit and visibly shaken.

"Strike two," he said to himself.

He had to convince the two soldiers that he was okay as they helped him back down from the ledge. But then he asked the unit's CO to cordon off the little building and guard it until someone from the *USA* could look inside.

A moment later, St. Louis' radio beeped. It was Roy. He was about 1,500 feet below with the units trying to gain entry to the mountain fortress through the hole left by the B-52 drone strike.

All he said to St. Louis was: "Get down here quick . . ."

It took the Mayor about half the time to get down the mountain as it did to go up.

He'd borrowed a humvee and began driving like a madman. Once on the ground level, he made a high-speed dash down the very long runway, veering every dozen feet or so to avoid running over the bodies of the fallen YS soldiers.

His F-20s and the pair of KC-135 aerial tankers had landed on Disney by this time, further crowding the end of the main airstrip, but he finally reached the site of the B-52 drone crash in good order.

Much of the plane itself was gone. Some traces of the engines and the landing gear remained, but everything else had vaporized. The old Buff had done its job, though. The door to the hidden fortress was enormous and thick. Highly polished, with giant bolts of steel sticking out all over, it looked like the door to Superman's Fortress of Solitude. But thanks to the B-52 drone strike, there was now a 6 x 6-foot hole in it, dead center, about twenty feet up.

The LA soldiers had rolled up their C-5's access stairs. They just barely reached the hole in the side of the enormous steel door.

Roy met St. Louis at the bottom of the stairway. He appeared very down. There were also a couple dozen LA Army soldiers around the site; they too looked downcast and not relieved in any fashion.

Another bad sign.

St. Louis looked at his old friend and shrugged, as if to say: "What's up?"

Roy just pointed to the hole in the massive door. "Go see for yourself."

St. Louis took the stairs two at a time. This was supposed to be the crowning achievement of the Disney Island attack—gaining access to the mountain fortress and all that it held inside, including the Jumbo-Jumbo and its flock of drones.

It's what everyone wanted, the only real reason they even invaded this place.

He reached the top of the steps. A portable spotlight had been set up here. St. Louis took off his helmet and sunglasses, peered inside the hole—and almost collapsed.

"Goddamn . . ." he swore out loud this time. "Strike three . . ."

Chapter Thirty-Two

Thirty-six Su-34s from the USS *USA* had bombed Mirror Island just ten minutes after it had been evacuated.

Hawk Hunter, Bateri and the crew of the Ka-27 watched from atop Tatu's holy plateau as the volcanic isle nearby was transformed into a cauldron of dirty black smoke, punctuated by sudden flashes of bright orange flame, this whenever another Su-34 dropped its ten tons of ordnance onto the crater. With each explosion a geyser of shattered reflective glass, the last of the towering mirrors, would cover the island with yet another layer of what for all-the-world looked like millions of diamonds.

Hunter left Bateri in the care of his 22 villagers, while the Slugboats, the Hinds and the other Ka-27s were delivering the last of the Tannu warriors back to their home island. Bateri hated to see him go, but made Hunter promise that it wouldn't be so long next time before the gods came back to visit.

Hunter made that promise.

The carrier was now about 100 miles out from Tatu, steaming northeast.

All of the Su-34s from the Mirror Island strike had returned, all the Hinds and most of the Ka-27s had as well. Pressed into duty as both landing craft and recovery vessels, the last of the Slugboats were just ten minutes away.

It had been a long day, but finally the burning bright sun began to dip in the west. That's when Hunter's Ka-27 landed on the *USA,* the last helo to come onboard.

He and the crew made a quick visit to the starboard galley to get coffee, and then went their separate ways. The helo crew was off to secure their aircraft; Hunter went up to the war room.

Everyone was there—but they all stopped talking the moment he arrived.

He stood in the doorway for a moment, huge cup of coffee in one hand, a commandeered sugar dispenser in the other. It was as if someone was going to yell: "Surprise!"

But in the next instant, he knew what was really happening.

"We lost the 'coin flip?'" he asked them.

Grim nods all round.

He collapsed in the nearest empty seat.

"Son of a bitch," he moaned.

They'd invaded Disney Island with zero pre-strike intelligence on the target. Again, not the first time; the UA had run many big operations nearly blind.

Their hope was that with the B-52 drone strike, the Jumbo-Jumbo and any of its drones would be encased inside the fortress, eliminating them as a threat. But they also knew the chances of actually catching the gigantic airplane on the ground would be literally 50-50.

A coin flip . . .

They'd successfully completed all the other missions involved in the island-hopping campaign. And there'd been no losses because most of YS soldiers were dead before any battles could be fought. It had been an astonishing run of good luck—but Hunter knew now it had come to an abrupt end.

"The place was empty," Dozer told him, the ship's CO being the bearer of the bad news. "No Jumbo-Jumbo, no drones."

Coffee forgotten, Hunter sank even deeper into his chair.

"So, it's still out there," he groaned. "Flying around with all its little killer bees."

He looked across the planning table at Dozer and added: "They're going to hit us . . ."

"It's a definite possibility," Dozer replied, nodding glumly. "And we're getting ready for it. Now that everyone's on board, we're in complete lockdown. We're tied up tight and . . ."

He let his voice drift off.

Crunch spoke up. "You know, the mothership and drones could have deployed to a rear area somewhere," he said, not an unreasonable theory. "We made it uncomfortable for their buds. Maybe they decided to take a few days off."

"I wish," Hunter replied darkly. "But these Yellow Star guys—whoever they are—like doing things big, if just to make a point. If they still have the firepower, they're not going to let us get away with hitting them so hard."

The war room went silent. Each drone could carry at least 300 pounds in bombs and the swarm had made short work of the three dozen ships in the AMC fleet. Had those attacks been against the carrier, as they'd initially feared, it would have been catastrophic.

One big question now was: how many drones did the Jumbo-Jumbo mothership have left?

But no one had to ask it. All eyes went to Roy From Troy. His trained eyes had seen inside the mountain fortress.

"It wasn't just empty, Hawk," he explained. "There was a lot of evidence that this was where they manufactured the drones. And from the looks of all the machine shops inside, I'd say they were able to make a lot of them in a short amount of time. I should only have such a great facility."

"We've got to go on the assumption that there's another sizable drone fleet out there," Dozer added, "flying around with their mothership. And from the sounds of it, that Jumbo-Jumbo is big enough to have revolving flight crews. If so, they could stay aloft for days. And with aerial refueling, it gives them almost unlimited reach."

"Waiting for just the right time to hit us," JT said echoing the gloom in the room.

"And impossible to pick up on radar," Ben added.

Another dark silence.

Finally, Hunter said: "The drones are stealth, but their mother of a mothership isn't."

He turned to Dozer and asked: "Is the lockdown an NBC?"

Dozer nodded. As in nuclear, biological or chemical—the three biggest threats to any carrier. The procedure was to seal up everything on board as tightly as possible. All planes off the flight deck, all guns on the carrier manned and ready, fire teams and corpsmen standing by. Basically, the ship was on a war footing, which meant expect an attack at any time.

It was the logical thing to do, considering the circumstances.

"But when?" Frost asked, voicing what was on everyone's mind. "When will they hit us?"

Club the weatherman spoke up. "There's a large front chasing us across the Pacific; it has the building blocks to cause a cyclone. It will catch up with us at 2100 hours and it will be rough going at least until dawn. If these drones are expendable and the mothership can control them from hundreds of miles away, then, I have to tell you, some kind of an attack just before the bad weather really gets here would not be unlikely."

Hunter started to get up. "I'm going to get going then," he said.

All eyes went back to him.

"Going where?" Dozer asked him.

"Going up to look for the mothership," he replied matter-of-factly.

The room was more than slightly stunned. Even for the Wingman, taking off with a cyclone on its way was above and beyond.

"It's a lot easier to take care of the mother hen than a couple hundred—or even a couple thousand—drones," he explained to them. "I just need something to fly."

He turned to Ben and JT. "Can I borrow one of yours?"

They didn't answer right away, which was odd. Instead they looked at Dozer, who just threw up his hands. "What's the point in not telling him now?" he asked.

"Tell me what?" Hunter replied, completely baffled.

208

Ben and JT stood up and motioned to Hunter. "Follow us," Ben said.

Chapter Thirty-Three

When elements within the New Russian Empire first built the gigantic aircraft carrier, it had been christened the *Admiral Isakov.*

Its official designation was "aircraft-bearing battle cruiser," and while its air operations were the sexy part, the ship was a formidable battlewagon as well.

It had four gigantic turrets, each one containing three 18-inch guns, just one of which could fire a two-ton high-explosive shell up to 30 miles away. These turrets bracketed the ship's colossal ten-story superstructure. Further down the starboard weapons' deck, there were lines of SAM launchers, rotary cannons and CIWS Gatling guns.

On the port side, starting at the angled flight deck and going all the way back to the stern, this awesome array was duplicated—twice.

But there was no argument the carrier's greatest weapon was the F-16XL and the person who flew it.

Shot full of holes in his eternal dogfight with the Black Flanker and banged up during its "soft" landing afterwards, it was a mess by the time it was airlifted back to the boat.

But not unrepairable.

While Hunter was off the boat meeting Bateri and then dashing back to the Boneyard, a crew of Su-34 mechanics, working on their downtime, patched up the XL and got it back to flying condition—somewhat.

It wasn't one-hundred percent. Most of the cannon damage from the dogfight had been to the XL's nosecone, resulting in extensive burnouts to his cockpit control panel. Some of these avionics were destroyed beyond repair, but the air monkeys were able to perform a massive rewiring job and got the most important control panels back up and running.

The XL's bomb-dropping systems had been destroyed and it wasn't able to shoot Sidewinder missiles either. But the six-pack of M61 Vulcan nose cannons had been fixed and resighted. The monkeys had even found a way to add about fifty percent more in cannon shells to the ammo cans. The XL was loaded for bear.

Hunter found out all of this after Ben and JT took him from the War Room down to the maintenance deck and presented him with the dinged-up XL. The Wingman was floored. It was a great surprise, pulled off while his mind and body were elsewhere. He was speechless for more than a minute, which was not like him at all.

Most of the rest of the crew learned of the XL's resurrection only when the carrier's main aircraft elevator brought the dented superjet up to the flight deck. Had this been a movie, this would have been the scene where the ship's entire company appears up top and gives the plane and its pilot a rousing round of applause.

But the deck was clear of all but essential people at the moment. The carrier's other aircraft had been secured below. Only the XL would be going up this dark and stormy night.

The carrier's clean deck made the flattop look absolutely enormous, giving everything an otherworldly vibe. Hunter hooked up to the far port-side catapult, revved his massive engine, and checked the steam pressure reading. All was go.

He saluted the launch captain. Two seconds later he was thrown off the deck at 120 mph.

Putting the battered F-16XL on its tail, he went straight up into the night.

They'd worked on a plan—yet another plan—slapped together while he was suiting up for this flight.

All of the carrier's surface weapons were armed and ready. The mammoth 18-inch guns were loaded with huge 2,000-pound antiaircraft shells. When exploded, they filled the air with thousands of pieces of shrapnel, a cloud so dense few aircraft could survive being anywhere near it.

The SAMs were all calibrated for what was expected to be close-in firing, too. The same for the various Bofors AA guns and the dozen CIWS Gatling-style cannons, capable of firing 4,000 rounds a minute.

The plan said if and when the drone swarm got close, the ship would fire one mammoth fusillade at them, a concentrated wall of lead they were hoping nothing could get through.

The Su-34 squadrons, the Hinds and the Ka-27s could do nothing against the drone swarm; common sense would keep them below decks and out of the fray. But they would contribute to the battle as all the cannon rounds from all their onboard weapons had been stripped out and dispersed as extra ammunition for the ship's high-firing CIWS deck cannons.

This was more firepower than most navies around the postwar world. But after seeing what the drones did to the AMC just by sheer numbers alone, it all seemed lacking by comparison.

The UA needed another edge; something to keep them afloat until Hunter found the Jumbo-Jumbo.

As it turned out, they had one more ace in the hole: Tony 3.

The rotund filmmaker was entrenched in the war room with the rest of them, working the ship's main radio.

He was looking for a needle in an infinitely huge electronic haystack. Having pulled apart the YS drone they'd recovered after the AMC attack, he felt if he was privy to what radio frequencies the YS used, he might be able to break in on their microburst commands and . . . well it had not gotten any further than that, only because finding the right YS channel seemed impossible in the first place.

For whatever reason, the Yellow Star used radio frequencies in the 2290-2300 megahertz range. If there was an obscure place to land on the radio dial, this was it. Before the war, these frequencies were used primarily for one thing: deep space communications.

But very little of that had been happening since WW3.

The only plan Tony could come up with was for him to sit at the carrier's main radio, and using its touch panels, tap his way through all the transmission possibilities within 2290 and 2300, looking for the YS's elusive radio channel.

Chapter Thirty-Four

By the time Hunter took off, the entire carrier task force had turned east and was moving full speed ahead.

Ostensibly, they were heading back to LA, but everyone on board knew a drone attack was imminent. It said something about the collective consciousness of the crew that the prevailing mood actually found an upside to the situation. If the drones were going to attack, it might as well be now, before they got anywhere near LA.

Taking the hit out here could spare the American West Coast.

The carrier's defensive strategy gave the Slugboats an especially dire mission.

Known as Formation Picket-10, the twelve armed tugs were sent out ten miles in every direction, in practice, forming a loose security cordon around the huge ship. But in reality, they were going to be the carrier's trip wire.

Slugboat 7 was on the port forward flank; first in line on the left side. The *USA* was about ten miles off starboard, its enormous profile dominating the horizon even in the gathering darkness. The wind had picked up since the tug had arrived on station. The waves were getting choppy.

The storm was coming,

It had been a crazy forty-eight hours for Lt. Ruggeri and his crew. Colliding with the downed drone, dumping the AMC officer's body on Mirror Island, recovering Hunter and Tony 3 after the B-52 drone strike on Battery Island. Unforgettable moments, fraught with anxiety but weirdly mixed with exhilaration. The crew had learned a lot about adrenalin highs in the past two days.

But this moment was different. The tugs were out here as a crude early warning system, canaries in a coal mine. Because the drones didn't show up on radar, if the carrier was going to have any warning at all, it was probably going to require a visual sighting, from the tugs, at night, in increasingly high seas and the approaching bad weather.

A long way from perfect, but again that's what it had come down to.

Ruggeri's orders were grimly simple. If you spot the drone swarm, warn the carrier and the other tugs immediately, and then engage the enemy. No more needed to be said. Everyone on board the Slugboat knew the consequences of those instructions. If they spotted the drone swarm, then that probably meant the drones had spotted them. The tugs were tough, but just one of the kamikaze UAVs would be enough to blow the tough sea dog to bits.

All hands were on deck now except the technician and the engineer, whose battle stations were below, and the wheelman, who was steering the tug from the elevated pilot house. Everyone up top was wearing a flak jacket and navalized Fritz helmet. They were also equipped with M-16s and NightVision goggles, including the three gun crews. Slugboat 7 boasted a trio of double-barreled 57-mm Bofors autocannons, fierce weapons guaranteed to ruin anyone's day. With two guns up front and one on the stern, they could keep up a rapid rate of fire practically nonstop, until the ammunition ran out.

Slugboat 7 had been making forty knots since the big turn east, serious speed for any tug. It was not so great on the engines, but in order to do their mission, they had to keep up with the rest of the task force. Should they fall behind, they knew their friends would come to look for them and probably wind up getting them all killed. That had to be avoided at all costs.

Battling the spray and wind now, everyone on deck was looking up into the dark storm clouds, ready for anything. This was the part Ruggeri hated the most: the waiting. And that the anxiety of waiting for the attack might be as bad as the attack itself.

But as it turned out, they wouldn't have to wait very long.

They were on station not ten minutes when Ruggeri's forward gun captain called out: "There they are . . . dead west, two lines, coming right at us . . ."

Everyone's eyes went to 5,000 feet, the altitude of the last drone attacks. But then the gun captain added: "Down low, ten above the line."

Now everyone else leveled out their Nightvision goggles—and that's when they saw them. Two massively long waves of UAVs, hundreds at least, maybe even more than a thousand, about two miles away. Easily twice the number that had attacked the AMC fleet, they were flying just 100 feet above the water and moving at barely 120 knots, much lower and slower than the last time they'd been seen.

Ruggeri keyed his radio and calmly reported to the carrier and the other Slugboats what he was seeing. Then he told his men to get ready to fire. His engineer and technician had climbed up on the deck by now, M-16s in hand, getting ready to do battle. Even the wheelman in the pilot house had his side access window open, his M-16 resting on its sill.

Ruggeri was proud of them—especially since this was probably the end. They and the other portside Slugboats would shoot down as many UAVs as they could. But with each enemy wave being at least a half mile long, even knocking down a hundred drones would be like spitting in the ocean. That's how many they were seeing.

Plus, engaging the drones meant giving their positions away. And then *they* would become the targets. If a drone in the first wave didn't get them, one in the second wave surely would. And if past history meant anything, the drones made sure not to leave any survivors.

The first of the two lines of UAVs was a mile away now; the second wave was a half mile behind that. The drones' notorious buzzing noise had arrived with the wind, frightening in its own way and growing in volume.

Ruggeri was standing on the bow, his M-16 up, eyes on his NVGs. He yelled up to his wheelman to keep going, full speed and evasive, no matter what. Then he told his crew to remember to hold their positions—and then grimly wished them good luck. Accepting they were all going to die was one thing, but it was sure going to be an odd way to go. Out in the middle of the Pacific, battling a swarm of monstrous mechanical insects on their way to sink the greatest warship ever built?

You couldn't make this stuff up.

Another few seconds passed, but then something *very* strange happened. It was so bizarre, every man on Slug-boat 7 had a different version of what they saw. It would be the same for all of the tug crews on the portside picket.

Everyone saw the same thing happen, yet everyone had a different way of describing it.

Most everyone agreed on one thing: what happened was either the paranormal—or miraculous.

Just seconds before they were about to open fire on the drones, they saw a sort of fiery ripple pass right in front of the first wave. It was traveling so fast, it seemed to distort the air around the UAVs, giving everything a mirage-y look. One Slugboat crewman described it as "ripping the fabric of time." Others saw it as a miles-long bolt of red light that moved too fast for the eye to keep up with it. Still others thought some kind of otherworldly object was involved.

Whatever it was, it left a highly disruptive tailwind in its wake—and this was violently knocking the drones out of the sky. Some collided causing sharp aerial explosions; some just plunged directly into the sea. All went out of control though, like "unlocking a zipper" someone else said.

Because they were at the other end of the picket line from where this started, Slugboat 7's crew had whatever it was in sight longer than most. And in that microsecond before it went by them, Ruggeri was certain he saw not an alien spacecraft, but Hunter's XL superjet spinning madly in front of the mechanical flock.

That's what was knocking them out of the sky.

It all happened in just a few seconds. And just like that, the first wave of suicide drones was gone.

But there was still the second wave.

Many finally did see the XL once it stopped spinning and realized that it'd been Hunter who'd downed the entire first wave of drones without firing a shot.

But now, with the second wave bearing down on them and the carrier beyond, it's what people saw next that bordered on the unbelievable.

Because at this most critical of moments, when everything the Americans had fought for hung in the balance, they saw Hunter's superjet literally turn on its tail and leave the field of battle.

That was the low point for the crew of Slugboat 7.

No sooner had the exhaust flames of the XL disappeared into the murk, when it was like everything went into rewind, like the big cosmic clock had reset itself back a half minute or so.

Meaning they were facing the same death sentence, it had just been delayed a bit.

Far from being disrupted, the second wave was forming itself into an attack chevron—an enormous arrow in the sky, pointed directly at the USS *USA*—with only the port side picket tugs in between. Now that individual drones were coming into view, it was clear their wings were visibly drooping; they had to be carrying much larger bombloads this time, and that's why they were flying so low and so slow.

Ruggeri focused on one UAV and ID'd the ordnance as 250-pound naval penetration shells, two per drone. The grim math said if each drone carried 500 pounds of bombs, multiplied by at least *six hundred* drones meant 150 tons of high explosive was headed for the USS *USA*—at 120 mph. There was no way even a monster like the *USA* could survive that.

Everyone on Slugboat 7 got ready to fire again, darkly anxious now to get their final battle underway. But Ruggeri knew they had to be smart about it. He held up his hand, signaling them to wait.

The UAVs closed to less than a half mile. The combined buzzing was growing louder.

"Hold your fire . . ." Ruggeri warned his men. The closer their targets, the more of them they'd be able to get—before one got them.

"Hold . . . and check . . ." Ruggeri said again, the swarm now just 1,500 feet away.

Each man did a last check of his weapon.

A thousand feet away. The buzzing was now a banshee scream.

"Hold . . ."

Ruggeri found himself morbidly wondering which kamikaze would choose to hit their little armed tug, bringing them all down with it.

"Hold . . ."

The swarm was now just 500 feet away—and it was clear Hunter was not coming back to perform another miracle.

So, indeed, this *was* it.

"Let's make them proud!" Ruggeri heard himself shout. Then he called out: "In three . . . two . . . one . . . *fire!"*

The night was suddenly lit up with tracers as the Bofors guns and the M-16s opened up on the drones. It was so bright the ocean looked on fire and the cloudy sky, bright as day. Not a second later, all the armed tugs along the picket line opened up as well. Long, long streams of luminous rounds rose into the night. Dozens of drones were hit, dozens were going down.

But suddenly the UAVs were right on top of them. The buzzing noise was maddening, the gunfire blinding and intense. Ruggeri's wheelman was keeping the tug on its violent zigzagging evasive course with one hand, while firing straight up at the UAVs with his M-16 in the other. Even the technician and the engineer were blasting away. It was exciting and it was crazy. Ruggeri steeled himself, just waiting for one of the mechanical bugs to divert from its course and end it all.

But . . . it never happened.

The swarm went right over their heads. None of the surviving drones diverted from its course. Ignoring the Slugboats completely, they were quickly gone in the stormy night.

Ruggeri was stunned. They all were. He grabbed his radio and reported to the carrier what had just happened. "It appears they're programmed to hit the carrier," he told them urgently. "And nothing else."

It was only when those words came out of his mouth did Ruggeri realize he and his men might live after all.

But their friends on the carrier were probably not going to be so lucky.

Chapter Thirty-Five

Hunter had gone straight to 42-Angels after catapulting off the carrier, arriving there just thirty seconds later.

He leveled off and commenced a long slow orbit around the carrier. Nearly eight miles high, his plane's radar was burning red hot, sending out pings in all directions. But his own internal radar was ice cold.

He chose this height for a reason. The first time he'd spotted the Jumbo-Jumbo he was up here, and it was flying at 25,000 feet. It seemed like the right place to begin his search.

He was looking for what was probably the largest airplane ever built—how hard could it be? But the real question was, could he find it before the drone swarms began their attack on the carrier?

The answer to that question turned out to be no.

And that led to what happened next.

It was strange how fast it happened. One moment his radio was quiet. The next, a cascade of voices assaulted his eardrums. Numerous transmissions were suddenly bouncing between the carrier and the Slugboats. It could have meant only one thing.

The swarm had been spotted.

He'd just completed his first circuit around the carrier when the radio went nuts. Staying in his sharp bank, his plugin NVGs down and warm, he immediately saw the two very long lines of Yellow Star UAVs coming right at them.

Even in the ethereal glow of night vision the UAVs looked unreal. Never had they appeared so buggy-looking. And there were easily a thousand of them this time.

A split-second decision came next, one of several he would make tonight. He knew what he had to do—or try to do. The Slugboats on the port side picket line were about to engage the drones; he thought he could help them. What he had in mind had worked numerous times for him before, when he'd faced SAMs or air to air missiles or even other aircraft.

It was a physics thing. No shots required.

The next thing he knew, he booted in the afterburner, turned 180-degrees and started falling from 40,000 feet. It took him only a few seconds to get down to wavetop level. Then a twist to starboard, another to port—and just like that, he was looking down the line of the first wave of drones.

He just started spinning; again, it was as simple as that. Disrupting the air flow in front of any aircraft would give it problems. There was nothing paranormal or extraterrestrial about it. If he could knock some of the UAVs off course, it would make it easier for the guys in the picket boats and on the carrier beyond.

He'd managed to keep the XL spinning for the entire length of the first wave. It took all of three seconds on full afterburner. One hundred and thirteen revolutions in all.

But then he was as surprised as anyone when he looked back and saw he'd KO'd *all* of the UAVs in the first wave. The collisions, the death dives into the ocean, all of them out of control—it was totally unexpected. But it proved one thing in his mind: the drones' radio-controlled flight programs were even more rigid than they'd thought. Disrupt one tiny element and the rest goes haywire.

Fueled that he'd finally found a way a fighter pilot could attack these things, he was about to burner up again, loop an up-and-over—and do the same to the second wave.

But then his body began shaking from boots to helmet and back.

It was the *feeling*—and he immediately recognized this particular sensation. Something was out there. Something big and flying.

He roared up to 5,000 feet and leveled off. Time froze—and now it seemed very real. He closed his eyes and beseeched the cosmos to help him—to help them. Just a simple message came through at first: look down. He did as he was told, and peering through his NVGs at the dark storm clouds below, he suddenly saw an opening at around 2,000 feet, with the very choppy sea beyond.

But what he saw next was a heart-shaped island— causing his breath to catch in his throat. He blinked and the peephole went away, but only to have another one open up just a few seconds later. Now he believed he was looking down at a fog-enshrouded island.

He aggressively shook away these thoughts—he knew where they were going.

He shut his eyes and tried a third time. When he opened them, he was again looking down at a huge patch of ocean. And flying along at just 2,000 feet was the Jumbo-Jumbo.

And this time, it really *did* look like a whale in flight.

He looked down at his radar just to confirm what he was seeing. The big plane's electronic signature was so huge it took up a third of his screen.

At that moment, the cosmos started ticking normally again, just in time for him to realize he had a heart-wrenching decision to make.

Should he pursue the flying whale? Or double back and take care of the second wave of UAVs?

At that moment, his radio exploded again with the news that the second wave had at that moment passed over the picket ships—and had kept right on going.

That made it easier for him to decide. The killer drones were indeed rigidly programmed, and for this mission, they were rigidly programmed to hit the carrier—and nothing else. That's why the picket tugs had been saved.

So he *had* to turn back and try his spinning distortion trick again to save the carrier. The Jumbo-Jumbo would have to wait.

But just as his hand began to move the controls, he received another message from on high, a tidal wave of the *feeling* washing through his body.

He had never felt it so strongly. And his cosmic, super-gut instinct was telling him to go after the Jumbo-Jumbo instead.

There was a kind of logic behind it: Destroy the Jumbo and you destroy the drones. Destroy just the drones and the Jumbo was still out there.

It seemed to make sense now.

But he hadn't been to sleep in days.

There was a problem right away. With no air-to-air missiles to count on, he had only his six Vulcan cannons to take on the aerial leviathan. True, he had fifty percent more ammo than usual and most things he'd shot down over the years rarely took more than a couple well-timed, well-placed bursts from the Six-Pack.

But he knew this time would be different.

He put the XL into a sharp drive and on reaching 2,500 feet, opened up on the Jumbo-Jumbo with his half-dozen cannons. The two luminous streams of tracer rounds took a winding, twisting path to their target—but then he saw dozens of puffs of fiery red light up both of the big plane's tail sections. He rocketed right by the Jumbo two seconds later, just in time to see large chucks of both tail wings disappear into balls of flame.

But the Jumbo-Jumbo just kept on going, not diverging from its original course for even a moment.

Hunter knew right then that this was going to be harder than he thought.

He bottomed out at 1,000 feet, did another rapid climb, finally flipping over at 3-Angels. A quick shallow dive put him back on the Jumbo's six.

He fired once again. And once again, he scored two direct hits, this time on the plane's starboard outer wing. Two more large pieces of the aircraft broke away—and the plane actually staggered a bit.

But only for a moment. It quickly restabilized itself and then kept right on going.

Hunter felt a distinct horror run through him. What if he'd made the wrong decision? Maybe he should have taken out the drones first.

Again, he looked down at his gigantic target, flying straight and level, barely affected by his four direct-hit cannon barrages.

Pushing the throttles ahead, he tried it two more times. Two more loops, two more pinpoint hits to the double-747's tail sections and outer wings.

But, again, to no noticeable effect.

The big plane just kept on flying.

"God damn," Hunter swore finally. "Now what?"

Chapter Thirty-Six

Tony 3's hands were moving so quickly, even he couldn't keep up with them.

This had nothing to do with little green pills. This was all him, moving at superhuman speed and wondering if he was in some kind of bad dream.

He was still sitting front and center at the main communications console inside the carrier's war room. A crowd of very concerned officers and crew were jammed in behind him. All eyes were fixed on the room's huge TV screen.

It was showing the second wave of drones. They were heading right for the carrier's broadside and no more than a minute away.

Tony was pushing two different lighted panels on the communications console with lightning speed. With each push, he was listening in on a separate radio frequency he knew the Yellow Star might use; this after he'd studied the receiver found in the killer drone the UA recovered after the AMC attacks.

Again, the problem was the YS used the very unusual radio frequencies in the 2290 and 2300 megahertz range to communicate. Before the war, these channels were almost exclusively used for deep space radio communication. And because there were hundreds of possible channels between 2290 and 2300 that the drones could be attuned to, the only way to find out was to listen in on all of them until he hit upon the one he was looking for.

But everyone in the war room knew they were facing a disaster here. They'd all heard the ominous warning from Slugboat 7, that the drones were carrying even larger bombs than before. The next thing they heard, the armed tugs were shooting at the UAVs as they were going over their heads.

But then the communications line went dead.

The seconds ticked away. Tony's fingers continued moving at high speed, but the swarm would now be here in less than a minute. Although Bull Dozer was right next to him, Tony was so involved in what he was doing he didn't hear the CO's order for the ship's company to open fire on the drones. It was going to be one, gigantic barrage, fired in very close.

It came as a single, overwhelming, ear-splitting *bang!* as all of the carrier's heavy guns fired at once. The result was hellish and blinding. The simultaneous blast of the twelve 18-inch guns rocked the giant ship from side to side. The huge 18-inch antiaircraft shells exploded just 2,000 feet out from the carrier—and they were absolutely frightening, like little nukes blowing up in space. Add in all the other weapons being fired—the SAMs, the Bofors twin-barrels, the CIWS Gatling guns—and it conjured up a nightmarish scene where nothing could possibly get through such a wall of fire.

Yet something did.

The smoke cleared and those in the war room were stunned to see about two thirds of the drones were still flying. They'd made it through their fusillade somehow, meaning at least a hundred tons of high explosive was still heading for the carrier, more than enough to turn the big boat into a flaming hulking wreck.

Tony could feel the last moments of his life ticking away. He didn't know what to do. He still had hundreds of frequencies to go through, and though his hands were still moving at a blur, there just wasn't enough time left to find the right one.

But then he had a strange last thought, a memory from when he was young. He'd had an argument with his mother on whether guardian angels were real.

She believed they were; he didn't.

Now he heard himself whisper: "I wish I had one now . . ."

Two things happened in the next instant. He remembered looking up at his own reflection in the glass of the TV screen and seeing the slightly distorted image of the crowd of crewmembers behind him, breathlessly watching the drama. Among them was a young girl who stood out because she dressed casually in jeans and a white baseball cap.

He remembered thinking it was an odd time to be out of uniform.

In that same moment, the frequency he'd clicked onto started howling with white noise and electronic beeps, with a very robotic-sounding voice trying to be heard above it all.

He'd done it.

He'd found the frequency the YS used to control its drones.

The killer bugs were about thirty seconds away now. Tony hastily opened up an audio link and started yelling: "Abort! Abort!"

He hadn't planned for this part because he never thought he'd get this far. "Abort" was the only thing he could think to say.

But it was not enough for the killer drones to break off the attack.

However, it did do something . . .

The eyes of everyone in the room were fixed on the approaching UAVs, now less than two football fields away. Then in a day of many surprises, something else completely unexpected happened: the swarm suddenly dropped their bombs. They fell into the sea, many of them exploding on impact.

Those in the war room couldn't believe it. Tony's plan had worked . . . sort of. Whatever their electronic ears had heard from him, it caused the UAVs to drop their payloads prematurely.

But while the drones were no longer carrying any ordnance, they were still heading right for the carrier.

They started slamming into the flight deck seconds later. Even without their bombs, each impact sounded like a bundle of dynamite going off. The drones weighed a few hundred pounds each and they still had fuel in their tanks, so when they hit at 120 mph, it was with substantial force and caused substantial explosions.

First there were dozens, and then hundreds. Within seconds, impact blasts were going off up and down the length of the ship. The quarter-mile long flight deck, the skyscraper like superstructure, the mammoth turrets— nothing was spared. Once again, the mighty ship began rocking violently from side to side.

It seemed to last forever—or at least nearly a minute for all of the 600-plus drones to hit the carrier.

But then, just as suddenly, it was over.

The flight deck was aflame from bow to stern and the wreckage of the drones was piled more than ten feet high in some places, sending out choking clouds of smoke.

But the USS *USA* was still afloat.

The crowd in the war room broke out in spontaneous cheers and applause, their sense of relief was palpable. Everyone was breathing again,

Tony turned to Dozer. They were both drenched in sweat. Their ears were ringing. Their hands were shaking.

"Muthafucker," Tony yelled to him. *"Now* is it over?"

Chapter Thirty-Seven

Hunter saw three separate explosions coming from the direction of the USS *USA*.

He was down at 5,000 feet about 12 miles north of the carrier, still pursuing the Jumbo-Jumbo, still pouring cannon fire into it, but still to no effect.

The first explosion had to have been the ship's entire arsenal firing at the drone swarm. The shock wave from this barrage was so extreme it shook the XL even though he was a dozen miles away.

The second series of blasts happened right off the carrier's port side. Something enormous must have exploded out there, because it literally blew a huge hole in the ocean, instantly turning millions of gallons of salt water into steam.

The third series of explosions was the most horrific; he imagined they were caused by the drones slamming into the carrier. As seen through his night vision goggles, the resulting flash was a complete washout of fiery green light. Something that would happen if a real nuke had gone off.

All communications with the carrier died a moment after that.

Time froze for him again, but not in any pleasant way. He tried reconnecting with the *USA* but with no luck, everything was fried on their end. When he looked over his shoulder, all he could see was a cumulus cloud of black and red smoke with towers of flame shooting out of it and rising high into the night. On night vision, it looked like the entire ship was on fire.

So he'd fucked up.

He'd trusted his cosmic instincts, and they turned out to be wrong. Had he gone after the second wave as he'd first intended, he would have at least lessened the massive hit he knew the carrier must have taken.

Despair washed over him. He found himself sinking into a black hole the likes of which he'd never known.

The ship . . . gone?

All his friends . . . *gone*?

But on a day *full* of the unexpected, there came yet another twist.

Suddenly, his communications snapped back on. Suddenly, his headphones were filled with chatter, excited talk . . . and cheering.

It was a true WTF moment, but somehow, the ship had survived. He didn't know how, but these were not the sounds of people on the verge of sinking or losing their lives. Relaxed laughter and a lot of cheering—that's what he was hearing.

But then, it was almost as if someone on the Jumbo-Jumbo heard it too, because suddenly the monstrous plane started changing course. It began veering to its right, the start of a long wide-out turn which, if completed, would bring its nose around so that it was pointing right at the bow of the carrier.

A million things went through his head on seeing this, none of them very clear. He'd been firing his cannons madly at the giant but still, so far, to zero effect.

Now with this ominous turn, he realized probably his last chance to kill it was to kill the air crew. So he hit the burner, streaked over the double-747, did a loop and then pulled back on the throttles. Suddenly, he was face to face with the flying monster. But that's when he realized something else: The plane had two tandem bodies which meant it had two flight decks.

Damn, he thought.

He'd have to do this twice.

He selected the port side flight deck first. Squeezing his trigger from about a thousand feet out, he directed his cannon rounds right through the canopy glass and into the flight deck. A series of quick, sharp explosions were the result.

Pull back on the stick, hit the burner again, another loop and he was staring down the Jumbo-Jumbo once again.

But it had nearly completed its own turn by this point, and just as he feared, it was lining up on the heavily smoking carrier.

He sent another hundred cannon rounds into the starboard side flight deck, leaving it exploding and in flames as well.

Pull hard again, another 5-g loop, another kiss from the burner and suddenly he was back where he had started, on the tail of the gigantic aircraft.

But nothing had happened. The plane had not diverted from its course one bit; it was still heading right for the carrier. In fact, it was speeding up.

What the hell was going on here?

He'd performed two flawless head-on attacks on the big plane . . . but nothing changed. He couldn't imagine either side's flight crew could have survived his onslaught.

Unless . . . there were no flight crews.

In that instant he realized something else he'd been missing all along. From the first time he'd seen it, the Jumbo-Jumbo had always flown in the same way: Very methodical, almost robotic. And now, even with two flights decks on fire, it still looked completely under control.

That's when it hit him.

The Jumbo-Jumbo was itself a drone.

And now it looked like it was going to slam into the USS *USA*.

It was pure ego, but he actually thought that at least his cosmic message to go after the flying monster had been a good one. The big plane had been the Yellow Star's fail-safe system all along. If for some reason their multiple, prop-driven drone swarm didn't accomplish the mission, then the Jumbo-Jumbo would.

And he was sure that's what was happening right now.

He had about one quarter of his ammunition left.

The Jumbo-Jumbo was ten miles out from the carrier, still heading right for it, and now slowly descending in altitude.

The ship was maneuvering wildly in the dark, trying to zigzag to safety, but it was hard to move such a behemoth quickly. Still, this indicated that the carrier saw the threat coming at them. But they were not shooting back at it, at least not yet.

Why?

Maybe because they knew he was up here, he thought. And if that was true, what did that say about them?

He *had* to save them, but damned if he knew how.

The dark thought of ramming the jumbo plane popped into his mind. Completely taking out the flight deck containing the big drone's controls might put an end to it. But he wasn't sure—and he didn't want to die in a fruitless effort.

Besides, he thought grimly, I'd probably bounce off.

The plane was now about seven miles out from the carrier, turning even as the ship desperately tried to maneuver out of the way.

Hunter put the XL right above it, not a half mile separated him from the big plane's damaged twin tails. He looked down on it, black thoughts still in his head.

There was a morbid logic to it. If the 747 hit the carrier, then the XL wouldn't have a place to land anyway. And bailing out wasn't really an option because it would only delay his eventual demise. He was going to the bottom no matter what.

So where on the Jumbo-Jumbo could he hit with the XL and do the most damage?

His eyes focused in on the one section of the huge airplane that was the most atypical thing about it: the center wing. That place in the middle where the two planes were melded together.

If the monster had a weak spot, this was it.

The gigantic plane was within three miles of the carrier now. It was down to 1,000 feet, still descending and still turning to keep up with the carrier's evasive maneuvers.

Again, Hunter made another split decision. Again, he never really thought about it.

He just put the XL into a steep dive, and aiming for that center wing, unloaded his Six-Pack of cannon fire into it. He was remarkably calm in doing this, considering that he was soon diving on the plane so fast, he couldn't have avoided a collision if he tried.

They say your life flashes before your eyes, but, truthfully, he only saw four faces. His girlfriend, Sara. Viktoria Robotov. Dominique. And the strawberry blonde in the white baseball cap.

He closed his eyes and whispered: "Goodbye to you all . . ."

The Six Pack ran out of ammo a moment later.

But a moment after that . . . he heard an enormous *crack!*

The XL actually shuddered for a moment when it happened. He opened his eyes just seconds from colliding with the Jumbo-Jumbo on full afterburner, but once again, everything went into slow motion. He heard another huge cracking noise and then saw the big plane below him start to shake violently . . . and then split apart. Thanks to his last-ditch barrage, the double 747's huge center wing had ruptured and fallen in on itself.

"You're kidding me," Hunter whispered, unbelieving. "No freaking way . . ."

But that's what happened. The center wing snapped, and the two separate fuselages fell off to either side. Watching them part like the Red Sea, Hunter steered the XL right through the newly created opening.

The two halves of the huge airplane continued flying for a short while—the ultimate nightmare scene for anyone watching. But finally they began falling. They both hit the water at just about the same time, not 100 yards off the bow of the *USA*.

This caused two powerful tsunamis, one of which hit the port side of the carrier, nearly capsizing it. Only that the second wave then hit its starboard side, counteracting the first that a catastrophe was averted. The flight deck was on fire in spots, though, and the enormous ship was still rocking back and forth, causing anything aboard her not tied down to become airborne. It seemed to go on forever—the crashing, the mechanical groans, the warning klaxons echoing into the darkness.

But eventually the big ship righted itself and stayed that way.

And then everything was calm again.

Chapter Thirty-Eight

The sun came up over the Pacific and a new day began.

Hunter and his battered XL were back aboard the carrier, landing with the help of both the arresting cables and an emergency metal mesh fence stretched across the deck, so little of the ship's big flat top was free of debris for landings.

The *USA* was a mess inside and out, but the engines still worked and within an hour of the battle's end, they were steaming eastward at fifty knots, once again, heading for home.

Everyone on board had been up for at least 24 hours or more, but no one wanted to go to sleep now. No one could. Small, spontaneous celebrations popped up all over the ship. Hunter and his pilot friends took over their favorite corner of the ship's starboard galley and began gorging on stew and the ship's brutal, but effective, home-brewed beer.

As was usually the case after a few cups of the high octane lager, the discussion turned to their greatest air battles—but this time it was with a twist. The entire threat of the Yellow Star, whoever they were, their drones, their mothership, their slave empire in the Solomon Islands, was defeated this day . . . by air power, flown by fighter pilots.

So, maybe *this* might be their greatest air victory of all.

"Fighter pilots don't fade away," JT said, as a toast for their sixth round of beers. "We just adapt . . ."

The war stories went round about their latest campaign and their roles in it, as more beer was brought on and more stew was to be had. Finally, those gathered egged Hunter on about what he considered his greatest individual mission—before this one, of course.

He didn't even have to think about it. Six months ago, in the middle of the night, in the middle of a firestorm, he sank super-villain Viktor Robotov's nuclear sub in the Elbe River as it was trying to escape the flames of Russian-occupied Hamburg. That one act rid the world of one of the vilest human beings ever. The misery he'd brought down on the planet while embarking on his various demented schemes to enslave humankind was immeasurable. As UA intelligence had always maintained that the supervillain's sub never went anywhere unless he was aboard, losing him represented a big check in the win column for them.

"Right down the middle," Hunter said, explaining how his cannon barrage had split Viktor's U-boat in two in a matter of seconds. "Right time, right place . . ."

*****

More beer, more stew, there was even talk about finally holding a parade in LA. Hunter was still buzzing through the afternoon, but by 1800 hours, he knew it was time to pull the plug and somehow made it to his quarters.

He was feeling no pain, but something else was building inside him. An odd kind of excitement. He was alive at the end of this very long day—they all were.

And now, for the first time in a long time, he actually wanted to go to sleep, wanted to dream. Wanted to see her again.

But not an instant after his head hit the pillow, the cabin phone rang.

It was Dozer. All he said was: "You're needed in the war room."

Then he hung up.

Hunter found an odd mix of characters waiting for him.

Dozer was on hand, so was Tony 3.

But also, there was Louis St. Louis and Roy From Troy.

The Football City F-20s, as well as the LA Army contingents in their C-5s and the tankers, were all on their way back to the U.S.

But St. Louis and Roy had stayed behind.

And from the expression on everyone's faces, Hunter knew it wasn't to deliver good news.

"Just tell me," he said wearily. "I'll believe anything at this point."

Dozer was shaking his head. "Maybe not this . . ."

They directed him to a seat in front of the room's large TV screen. Dozer nodded to Tony, who began a videotape.

It started out shaky, taking a few moments to settle down. But then Hunter realized he was looking at video shot from the interior of a humvee as it was climbing the road to the top of the fortress mountain on Disney Island.

"I started to get worried when I saw all the AA sites on Disney Island were automatic," St. Louis told him. "Just like at that secret weapons factory in Siberia, built by you know who."

"At the same time, I was looking through the hole in the fortress door," Roy added in his deep raspy voice. "And I'm finding the place empty."

St. Louis directed them back to the TV screen.

"And that's when I came upon this place," he said.

The video showed a small shack at the peak of the mountain, then guarded by LA Army troops. Hunter recognized the outside as some kind of radar transfer station, a place where data was backed up.

But this was a façade.

The video continued, leaving the vehicle and entering the shack. What was inside was a real eye-opener.

That shack didn't contain just some auxiliary piece of equipment. It turned out to be the center of operations on the entire island.

"Every order about running the island came through here," St. Louis explained. "All of it via remote control, all of it from somewhere else. Flight schedules, construction schedules, combat training—everything coming and going, it was all tracked from here."

The video panned the inside of the shack showing about a dozen small TV monitors hanging neatly on three of the four walls. Dominating the fourth wall were the controls for the gigantic radio receiver which took up most of the shack's floor space. It looked elaborate and oddly stylized, like it was from another world.

"Like Louie just said," Dozer began. "Whatever else these people were involved in, lots of stuff on the island was either automatic or run by remote control, including their zombie soldiers. But their means of mastery wasn't anything fancy. It was that odd-looking radio. Just look at how they were using it."

"Everything goes out in microbursts from one central location somewhere," Tony explained. "And when I say somewhere, I mean with the radio frequencies they use, it could be *anywhere* on Earth. But whoever's behind it uses radio like I've never seen. All the remote control weapons on Disney Island. The Jumbo-Jumbo. The soldiers on Disney. They all had the same little radio receivers imbedded in them, they all received microbursts telling them what to do."

"Man, it's a crazy world out there," Hunter breathed.

"It gets a lot crazier," Tony went on soberly. "The radio frequencies the YS used for their drones and the Jumbo-Jumbo were unusual, but not unknown. This was a good thing because it helped us stop them, once I hit upon the one they were using.

"But these transmitters we found on the dead YS soldiers: they weren't just sending radio signals to the brain, the transmitters were actually being *powered* by the radio waves. There were no batteries, no magical electric currents involved. They used ELF, radio waves we know can travel long distances. But apparently the Yellow Star was also able to make them carry electrical power within the radio signal and I've never heard of that kind of technology here before."

"'Here' where?" Hunter asked him. "Here on Earth, you mean?"

No one said a word.

Finally, St. Louis broke the silence.

"That's still not the worst of it, Hawk," he said, turning to Tony again. "Might as well show him now . . ."

Tony shrugged and changed out the video tape cassette for another one, unmarked.

"It's a good thing our guys didn't bomb that little shack in the video," he said. "Because it's provided a wealth of intelligence for us. Like we said, the Yellow Star kept an account of everything that went through the place. Every order from on high, every in-flight refueling for the Jumbo-Jumbo, down to what everyone was eating on the island that day. It was all kept on video, in a video bank, inside this shack. That's the data it was storing. That's what you're going to be looking at right now."

Tony started the recorder playing. It showed a video of a raw daily briefing that had been sent to the shack containing orders for all YS personnel on the island. The video was date-marked two weeks earlier, nearly a week before the UA Pacific patrol had even started.

But because it was a raw feed, the video actually began before the briefing got underway. Thirteen men were sitting around a planning table not unlike the one in the carrier's war room. Twelve of them were Asian and wearing Yellow Star officers' uniforms, though no ski masks were in sight. The thirteenth man's back was to the camera, and from the looks of the video set-up, it was never intended for his face to be broadcast. But it was clear just by the tone of the others around him, this person was the person in charge.

A conversation was going on concerning something on its lighted board. At the same time, a column appeared on one side of the video and started showing hundreds of different radio number combinations. They looked to be the codes the YS would be using that day.

It soon became obvious that the broadcast was somewhat staged as the uniformed men, all dressed in yellow and red military suits, moved awkwardly at times. It was also obvious that the man with his back to the camera was the only one speaking loudly.

But that voice . . .

That's when Tony stopped the tape, fiddled with some controls and then started it again. He'd been able to zoom in, not on the unseen man's face, but on his reflection in the top of the lighted table.

Hunter took one look, then dropped his head and started shaking it slowly, never saying a word.

So this is how the adventure ends? he thought.

It didn't make sense, but these days not many things did. These days, it seemed that as soon as you felt certain about something, well, that was the moment it was going to fall through. That when you thought you saw, just for an instant, a little bit of light peeking through the dark clouds, well, that was when the hole was going to close up and it would start raining again.

And just when you were convinced you killed the monster, that's when the monster comes back.

No, not many things made sense these days.

Because the man shown clearly in the reflection, wearing the uniform of a Yellow Star high general and looking very much alive and well, was Viktor Robotov.

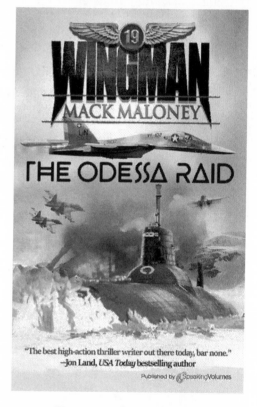

On Sale Now!

Codename: Starman *series*

For more information
visit: www.SpeakingVolumes.us

On Sale Now!

For more information
visit: www.SpeakingVolumes.us

On Sale Now!

WW III *series*

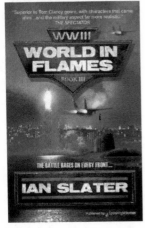

For more information
visit: www.SpeakingVolumes.us

Made in the USA
Middletown, DE
06 August 2020